Praise for

D0441214

"A dark, unforgettable tour inside the belly of the Hollywood beast. Novak knows this world, and it shows."

—D. B. Weiss, creator of HBO's *Game of Thrones*

"Actually funny."   —Peter Bart, *Variety*

"A slit-wrist wit that invokes the best of Bruce Wagner, with a sweetness in the darkest corners that calls to mind the late, lamented John O'Brien. But Novak's voice is all his own."

—Jerry Stahl, author of *Permanent Midnight*

FREAKS
OF THE
NDUSTRY

MEGAN—
NO COVERAGE!

—ADAM

FREAKS OF THE INDUSTRY

Adam Novak

A Barnacle Book | Rare Bird Books
Los Angeles, Calif.

THIS IS A GENUINE BARNACLE BOOK

A Barnacle Book | Rare Bird Books
453 South Spring Street, Suite 302
Los Angeles, CA 90013
rarebirdbooks.com

Set in Minion
Printed in the United States

10 9 8 7 6 5 4 3 2 1

Publisher's Cataloging-in-Publication data
Names: Novak, Adam David, author.
Title: Freaks of the industry / Adam Novak.
Description: First Trade Paperback Original Edition | A Genuine
Barnacle Book | New York, NY; Los Angeles, CA: A Barnacle Book;
Rare Bird Books, 2017.
Identifiers: ISBN 9781945572067
Subjects: LCSH Motion picture industry—Fiction. | Hollywood
(Los Angeles, Calif.)—Fiction. | Washington (D.C.)—Fiction. |
Scandal—Fiction. | Humorous stories. | Thriller fiction. | BISAC
FICTION / Humorous / General
Classification: LCC PS3614.O9253 F74 2017 | DDC 813.6—dc23

For Josh Gilbert and Karen Glasser
—slipped away to the next room

Human life is but a series of footnotes to a vast obscure unfinished masterpiece.

—Vladimir Nabokov

PHONE SHEET

SIN UTERO

SUICIDE BOMBER
GOES HOLLYWOOD

NAKATOMI PLAZA ATTACKED!

CENTURY CITY—A suicide bomber destroyed powerhouse talent agency Omniscience/Ragnarök, killing 167 agents and seriously injuring hundreds of assistants in what police are calling an act of "Westside terrorism."

An LAPD spokesperson said a suspected jihadist taxi driver was held, questioned, and released. Department of Homeland Security officials have yet to confirm the existence of a confession video or the identity of the bomber.

A rep for Justice for Janitors declined to comment.

SUPERSTAR
Screenplay by Manley Halliday

Ugly death, ugly life in this nasty biopic of Savannah, whose alcoholism, brash personality, and tragic demise make for an extremely compelling portrait of a superstar. Stronger than a Lifetime pic, more artistic than an *E! Hollywood True Story* episode, ambitious script paints Savannah with surreal touches that elevate an erratic life of botched plastic surgeries, cocaine addiction, and creepy fans. Like Frances Farmer (an institutionalized/lobotomized actress portrayed by Jessica Lange in *Frances*, which this most resembles; nothing's changed in showbiz*), SUPERSTAR is about a troubled performer accepting she's doomed, battling demons, spending the last year of her life with a shady male hustler who tries to help, but even he can't save Savannah from defeating herself. A diva and a drunk, hideous, gorgeous, unbelievably selfish, this isn't about redemption or providing any transcendent moments other than the theatricality of watching a porn star stomp herself out of existence.

showbiz

At every movie studio, whenever there's a regime change, the new studio chief is given three envelopes by her predecessor: "Open the first when you're in a jam, the second when you're worried, and the third when you're fucked," says the outgoing studio head. A few months later, the disaster movie *Volcanic* ($150M budget/$38M worldwide cume) green-lit by the previous regime fizzles at the box office. Rumors fly about studio stability, so the new chief opens the first letter in her desk drawer: "Fire the head of marketing." She gets rid of the well-liked marketing president and things calm down. A year later, the space oddity *Warlords of Arkadia* ($200M budget/$16M worldwide cume) crash lands on July Fourth with such a thud not even the forces of Subway and Burger King can halt the casualties. The studio chief opens the second letter: "Fire your president of production." After another year of embarrassing flops, the studio is considered a bomb factory, agencies send their clients elsewhere, and the town calls her kaput. The studio chief opens the last envelope: "Write three letters."

FACE LIFT*
Screenplay by Randy Flagg

Gripping actioner with moments of familial drama and a terrific concept about face-switching could connect with the masses. Smart script has cop Leo Walsh receiving a face-transplant of his worst enemy, Abel Caine, the psycho who killed his son, in order to infiltrate a downtown jail as Caine and prevent a dirty bomb set to go off somewhere in Los Angeles. The real Caine escapes from a state penitentiary, acquires Leo Walsh's face, and proceeds to usurp his life. Walsh, with Caine's face, busts out of an impenetrable prison cell, stops Caine from killing his unsuspecting family, and reclaims his identity. In the end, the cop wins but script hints it might be the psychotic Caine who wears Walsh's face. Engaging, huge in scope, clever concept is bolstered by brawny writing. Emily Walsh is a colonic technician still grieving the loss of their son who realizes her husband is not really her husband. Promiscuous teenage daughter Talley joins a Latino street gang, desperately needs eldering, only to receive the worst possible guidance from the lunatic masquerading as her Dad. It's Walsh's family portrait that stands out, just as the marital battle scenes elevated *True Fibs*. We should be all over this for our directors looking for a fine piece of action.

Face Lift

VP Rodney Muir leaves 20th Century Fox for a senior VP job at Paramount after supervising the monster hit *Face Lift* ($32M budget/$480M worldwide cume). Attending a drug-fueled bachelor party for his brother Scott in their hometown of Washington, DC, Rodney meets Thør Rosenthal, a North Hollywood-based filmmaker and requests a link to watch one of his no-budget movies (the wedding was called off; Scott would later be named White House press secretary after the suicide of Bob McAtee).

Alone at the hotel, Rodney decides to watch Thør's latest horror film, *Deathbed*. One room. One night. One angle. A young couple thinks their mattress is haunted so they set up a video camera in the corner of the bedroom to record all the freaky shit that happens to them after 3:33 a.m. Turns out it's not the mattress that's disturbed, it's the girlfriend, whose family had a death curse put on them for generations by a legendary witch in Roanoke, Virginia. Rodney thought the movie was raw but the idea had potential. He calls the director to say business affairs at Paramount would be making an offer to buy the genre film. Thør tells Rodney his ideas for a *Deathbed* quadrilogy; *Deathbed* duvet covers, *Deathbed* pillowcases, and a promotional tie-in with Mattress Discounters. Rodney humors Thør, never revealing his intention to remake the title and blast the original into outer space.

Rodney's splashy arrival at Paramount coincides with the announcement of a development deal remaking an untitled

DIY horror film with Vince Vaughn and Reese Witherspoon attached to produce and star. Rodney commissions several scripts and they all came in terrible. None of them kept the fixed camera conceit of *Deathbed*; "jump scares" were added, along with a needless backstory explaining the house was once a troubled orphanage that burned to the ground in a suspicious fire.

The senior VP visits Paramount's head of distribution Steve Bosco and begs him to hold a test screening for *Deathbed* at the Arc Light in Sherman Oaks. When the audience cards come back, Bosco orders Rodney into his office as if the executive had shit the bed. Bosco says he has never seen such scores in his life. *Deathbed* got a 92 percent score. Rodney silently thanks the Movie Gods. Bosco says he only pays attention to the combined score of the top two boxes ("Excellent" and "Very Good") and the "Definite Recommend" box. *Deathbed* received a deflating 4 percent top two box score and a "Definite Recommend" score of 2 percent. Rodney asks about the 92 percent and Bosco says: "Ninety-two percent said the picture was poor."

Rodney remembers the old saw that nothing good ever happens after four in the morning and no horror movie sprung from the legs of a stripper at a bachelor party ever gets a theatrical release.

FLEA FLICKER
Screenplay by Ben Sanderson

Engaging, blackly comic, dimensional script set in the barbaric world of the NFL. These football players are likely to be brain-damaged*, but man, are they hilarious. Like a bruised kid brother to *North Dallas Forty*, this is a wicked combination of gallows humor and underdog sports movie. Hero Wade Rypien is a rookie starting quarterback who struggles with crippling gonorrhea, devastating knee injuries, a severed ear, and back-to-back concussions while leading his team to the Super Bowl. Script succeeds in creating an "inside" look at the professional game, with an unflinchingly honest portrayal of the team owners as heartless capitalists, the league's rampant drug use (both recreational and medicinal), and the players as modern-day gladiators sent to die a thousand deaths on the gridiron. Material is confidently executed, with chatter that drips with sarcasm, humor, and the occasionally deep observation. Ending is bittersweet with the unexpected death of Wade in the end zone after scoring the winning touchdown at the Super Bowl. Exuberant, even philosophical, this zany football movie pulls off its ambitious playbook with subversive glee.

brain-damaged

Passed over during a regime change, Rodney leaves Paramount to run development for Bellerophon Pictures, a new film financier and independent distributor, when a dead hooker turns up in the backyard Koi pond of Bellerophon CEO Benny Pantera's Bel Air mansion.

Lebanese-born car wash mogul Pantera is best known for his lavish properties labeled "henhouses" providing shelter for desperate models/actresses, aka mattresses (part-time prostitutes who sell real estate, read scripts, and/or cut hair at salons on Canon Drive). Turns out the Koi pond victim lived at one of these henhouses until her skull was caved in by a lob wedge.

Deadline reports the dead hooker's sole credit on IMDb was "Dead Hooker" in *Plasma Sluts*, with a public statement from new production chief Rodney Muir released through his attorney declaring neither he nor anyone at Bellerophon had anything to do whatsoever with the dead girl found in the Koi pond, "on any level, personally or company-wise."

The letter ignites a multitude of protesters all day long waving signs ("*Plasma Sluts*") outside Rodney's Sunset Boulevard office, urging drivers stuck in traffic to honk in support of the slain prostitute, making any and all phone conversation impossible.

Police clear Pantera of any complicity regarding the murder on his property, but crude jokes at the mogul's expense through awards season (big laughs at the Oscars) discourages the town from doing any future business with anyone at Bellerophon Pictures.

Rodney resigns, swears off the industry, and moves back to Washington, DC.

MEMO

TO: LESTER BARNES
FROM: LARRY MERSAULT
RE: "IGNITION" // THOUGHTS
DATE: 4/22/13

IGNITION is off to a terrific start with intriguing characters and spectacular set-pieces. The setting of our nation's capital is as much of a star as our wheelchair-bound hero HARVEY CROSS. Next draft would be wise to develop more deeply everybody else who interacts with Cross, making this more of a relationship-driven actioner and a performance launch pad for Antwon Legion.

THOUGHTS:

—Remember what Mickey Rourke says to Kim Basinger at their first encounter in *9½ Weeks*? "Every time I see you, you're buying chickens." Cross and Lacey deserve a better first encounter; instead of giving them a "meet cute," consider having the wheelchair hero save Lacey, not the other way around, at the Washington Monument opener.

—Set-up needs a tighter focus on Harvey Cross undergoing a personal/professional downward spiral in Act I, setting the table for his last shot at redemption to stop the mad bomber.

———————MEMO———————

—Act II should have more moments of struggle, joy, and epiphanies for the suicidal Cross through his mentor/informant SKY KING, no-bullshit psychiatrist DR. BURGER, and the brewing chemistry with LACEY TORNADO, who provides him with a reason to live. Everything falls apart for Cross when Burger and Sky King get taken out by the mad bomber and Lacey is next on his kill list. Can he survive Act III by himself?

—Sometimes the police procedural stuff feels familiar; villain GRIMES could use more touches than his missing thumbs; script only hints at the dramatic possibilities of suicidal Cross and his by-the-book partner LACEY TORNADO. Script might be better off as a romantic two-hander with thoughtfully considered characters who end up saving each other.

—Second half after "good cop" Lacey gets suspended turns too dark too fast. Her descent into depravity, attempted suicide, and harrowing captivity mirrors too closely what Cross is going through.

—Consider reimagining Lacey after the suspension late in Act II; turning her life around; quitting drinking instead of drowning in alcohol; escaping captivity from Grimes and finding her inner "bad cop" to pay off the debt she owes Cross by rescuing his ass in the end.

MEMO

—For Antwon Legion, engaging action script continues to impress. Let's see what they do with the next pass.

Food for thought,

LARRY

WHERE'S THE BEEF?
Screenplay by Abraham Trumbo

Dry hamburger biopic of visionary salesman Dave Thomas and how he took a popular restaurant in Cleveland and turned it into the ubiquitous fast-food chain called Wendy's. Role of Dave Thomas is a fat, balding, fifty-something underdog, could be age-inappropriate for DQ, but still a potential signature part for any number of our clients. Dave's unsupportive spouse Suzanne is a bit one-note, probably not substantial enough to merit attention for Betsy Yarborough. Dull Madison Avenue squabbles and obnoxious Wendy's boardroom clashes swamp the engrossing narrative of underdog Dave Thomas and his brief triumph over McDonalds and Kentucky Fried Chicken. Best line of the script is when Dave Thomas is asked who came up with the catchphrase "where's the beef?" and Dave replies, "My wife." Script thinks the palace intrigue* of eighties burger wars is as compelling as *The Social Network* but it's not even close.

palace intrigue

Red and pink static in a circle; eye of an electromagnetic field; jolts of energy pulsing in his veins; flocks of birds morphing into white crucifixes, startling Antwon Legion from his onyx reflection in the bulletproof glass of the Hummer limousine.

Samoan bodyguards Fruity and Balthazar, formerly with Justin Timberlake, notice Legion flinch, decide it's nothing, go back to sharing a cherry blunt, filling up the cabin with ganja smoke. At least the movie star wasn't having a fitful nightmare about being crucified in Golgotha, which was heavy, and often. Legion takes a massive hit, coughs up a lung, plays with his Doberman, Bulgakov, as the Hummer rolls through Century City, past a homeless guy with a WILL SCREENWRITE FOR FOOD sign, arriving in front of Omniscience/Ragnarök.

Inside the mausoleum lobby, surrounded by every living soul of the agency, Lester Barnes welcomes the Stygian movie star with a fist bump. Legion appreciates their applause, his favorite sound in the world, all those subservient white faces making him the master, and they, his slaves.

GANGSTER, GANGSTER
Screenplay by Tyger McHenry

Think *Yojimbo N The Hood*. Stunning depiction of a twelve-year-old inner-city kid escaping his crime-infested community and finds a purpose to his meaningless life. Violent as any war film, unrelentingly grim, young hero Smoke fuels a bloody turf war between Spike, a heroin dealer who murdered his best friend and cocaine kingpin Snowball, who holds his sister Aliqua hostage in a crack house as a doped-up sex slave. Smoke stages a suicide mission to rescue his sister, killing Spike and Snowball, firing all of his ammo, including the extra bullet in his pocket he planned to use on himself if he were captured. Most moving scenes in this gang-related script are when Smoke and his uncle Juwon play Chinese checkers outside their public housing building to the background music of gunfire. Shocking epilogue will leave everyone breathless. A gritty take on *The 400 Blows*, the dialogue is profane but laced with wit and the power of street knowledge*.

street knowledge

Inside Omniscience/Ragnarök, Legion clutches his Academy Award for Best Original Screenplay, *I Am Legion*, relating his horrific childhood in abusive foster homes, a lifetime on the streets, and his rescue of an HIV-infected crack baby from drug dealers and indifferent bureaucrats.

As motion-picture, branded lifestyle, and television agents introduce themselves, the puffy clouds outside the floor-to-ceiling windows make the gathering celestial. Legion starts by giving thanks to his guru Lester Barnes for putting together *Ignition*, telling the room he can't wait to be on set with his director Thør Rosenthal and costar Betsy Yarborough.

The corporate consulting agents realize Legion's dream of being a Memphis barbecue sauce entrepreneur with the launch of "Brimstone BBQ" on fellow client Rachael Ray's cooking show; a Legion-inspired cologne will be offered exclusively at Macy's as well as a line of homeless-chic apparel in partnership with Target/Isaac Mizrahi. In addition to Legion's lucrative Claymation commercials for Coke Zero, a trio of book agents declare they have closed an eight-figure deal with HarperCollins for his inspirational tome FINDING ANTWON. Legion searches the room for the one person nobody thought to invite, his thousand watt smile disappearing—

"Where's reader-guy?"

The room has no idea who Legion is talking about. Unscripted TV agent Bramley Nazarian announces Legion will produce and star in a new ABC reality dating show where top sororities from the number one party schools in the nation compete against the Dallas Cowboys Cheerleaders, USC Song Girls, and famous MILFS like Kate Hudson and Jennifer Lopez to win his heart—

"People, we need to hit the pause button."

The room temperature turns Arctic; north of the eightieth parallel, everybody freezes.

"I need Larry Mersault in this meeting."

Fingers are snapped and an agent trainee is dispatched to retrieve the star's favorite minion.

LET IT SNOW
Screenplay by Clive Metzger

Movie on the page. Though script is a little bloated, every scene in this cocaine-fueled actioner crackles with unbearable tension. The smartest guy in a room* full of nutjobs, Jeb Huston gets arrested by the Feds, cuts a deal to save himself, betrays best friend Pablo Escobar, helps the DEA seize tons of cocaine smuggled into the country, gives up his sidekicks to prove his loyalty, marries a Colombian beauty who used to be Escobar's mistress, and plays both sides of the law against each other before jumping into the Federal Witness Protection program, where he lives today. Better than *Blow*, similar to *Goodfellas* with its terse narration and criminal behavior, bloodthirsty script offers a grimy canvas with plenty of car chases, blowjobs, and booger sugar; if this falls into Thør Rosenthal's hands, well, let it snow.

The smartest guy in a room

Wearing distressed jeans and a James Perse T-shirt with food stains that says "668: Neighbor of the Beast," Larry Mersault is greeted by Legion with a soulful dap followed by an elaborate secret handshake, with every agent in the room hatefully wondering what the fuck is going on.

The movie star places his reader between Fruity and Balthazar in the nosebleed seats behind the oceanic conference table. Legion causes a covering agent to blush when he thanks her for getting him a meeting with Spielberg. A senior agent with white hair raises a project at Universal his client is directing called "The Carthaginian" about the elephant-riding Hannibal that could be his *Gladiator*. When the star catches Mersault yawning, Legion declares he doesn't make movies with titles he cannot pronounce. Another agent, Korean, raises his hand. Lester Barnes nods, and the agent in Prada brings up Legion playing the heavy in the next James Bond installment. Lester suggests maybe MGM should consider Antwon as the next 007. Legion tells the room he doesn't want to play a villain, not yet, and he doesn't want to be James Bond—

"Are there any scripts out there about Jesus Christ?"

The room laughs, thinking Legion is fucking with them.

Larry Mersault raises his hand. The room goes quiet.

Mersault suggests an unproduced script called "Golgotha" by writer/director Thør Rosenthal.

The room detonates with dollar signs.

"It's *Se7en* meets *Last Temptation of Christ.* Pontius Pilate hires a private detective named Judas to investigate a serial killer who may or may not be the Messiah."

Legion hushes the room the way a quarterback silences a stadium.

"Is the script as good as *Faith Don't Leave*?"

"Better," says Mersault.

Legion steps around the flesh peddlers to Fruity and Balthazar sandwiching Mersault and raises the reader's paw like Buster Douglas in Tokyo—

"It's Miller Time."

JESUS CHRIST, THY NAME IS LEGION

TOLD YA! Oscar-winner **Antwon Legion** is attached to star in and produce faith-based feature "Golgotha" opposite **Seth Rogen** and **Michael Fassbender** for Bellerophon Pictures. Plot is being kept under wraps but it's believed to be a reboot of the last hours of Jesus Christ.

ANTWON LEGION

Omniscience/Ragnarök topper **Lester Barnes** says he's fielding eight-figure offer$ from distributors. "Golgotha" script will likely undergo a rewrite by the scribe-star.

The project was brought to Bellerophon by Omniscience/Ragnarök's **Larry Mersault**. Rogen and Fassbender are repped by Insanely Creative Artists. **Thør Rosenthal** directs.

MOO
Screenplay by Palmer Jessup

Based on a true story, *Silkwood* on a farm, so-so script relates the horrors of the beef industry and Big Agriculture's grip on our food chain. Unevenly written, sometimes this literal shit show of an industry can be riveting, but it's the people who disappoint. Kenny Barkley returns to his hometown as a lawyer for an Arkansas billionaire beef mogul after a viral video erupts about horrific bovine abuse. Anybody who attempts to expose the slaughterhouse is murdered and their death arranged to look like a suicide; Kenny discovers an industry-wide conspiracy of fattening the cattle to obscene levels, which causes the cows to cannibalize each other before they are clubbed to death; the farm's tainted milk causes birth defects, and the water in town is fecally poisonous. Kenny thinks he's found true love but he's been seduced by a Jezebel* secretly working for the beef mogul to gather information on him. Kenny blows the whistle, escapes with his life, but he can't save his farm friends. Ambitious script tries to be a suspenseful message movie and ends up being neither. Much a doo-doo about nothing.

Jezebel

White House press secretary Scott Muir grabs a drink with his notorious brother at Church and State on H Street to discuss his tsunami industry wipeout before attending the ceremony at the Irish Embassy on Massachusetts Avenue honoring their dad, a human rights activist recently awarded the Tipperary Peace Prize.

Scott is surprised to hear Rodney has already gotten a job at the Starbucks in Georgetown on Wisconsin Avenue like that Tom Hanks movie where the disgraced stock broker starts over as a barista with a bunch of misfit college kids serving decaf peppermint mocha lattes.

That night, after the medal ceremony, Rodney eyes a familiar redhead in a black mini-dress staring right at him, trying to place him; she, moving through the crowded embassy residence, he, brushing up against bare skin of backless dresses; everywhere Rodney looks, there she is, eye-fucking him like a vulture circling a motorist stranded in the Mojave Desert.

A sloppy drunk, his brother actually, blocks Rodney's view, raving about this "firecrotch" when he catches the enigma machine exiting the event. Rodney leaves his brother dissing the "ginger" immune to his charms, and cuts through the crowd, out the door, and there she is, bumming a cigarette from the valet guy—

"I can't let you pull a French Exit without getting your name."

"Maeve," she says.

"Is that your real name or your Starbucks name?"

She laughs, exhaling a cloud of regurgitated nicotine.

"You remind me of a guy I knew who ran from his apartment to my place with a six-pack of beer and a box of donuts."

"You remind me of this girl I never knew because I didn't run after her."

"I'm not going anywhere," says Maeve.

"You say that like you're doing a stretch in prison or something."

"Or married," she says.

"Ms. Macchiato," he snaps his fingers.

"I'm sorry?"

"That's what you always order at the Bux on Wisconsin."

Maeve flicks away her smoke. Rodney introduces himself.

"You're the reason I keep going back to that Starbucks."

"Is that right?"

"I like scars, Rodney. Do you have any?"

"Let's go upstairs and I'll show you."

Making out in a guest bedroom, Maeve and Rodney agree to postpone the inevitable and, still kissing each other, decide for propriety's sake he should return to the party first. Maeve waits five minutes and rejoins the event as if they hadn't just torn each other's clothes off. Imagine Rodney's shock when Ireland's ambassador to the United States, about to give a speech recognizing the peace efforts of the guest of honor, aka his father, takes a moment to introduce his second wife, aka Ms. Macchiato, face flushed, to the celebratory participants. Soon they are regularly steaming up the windows of her Range Rover in the Starbucks parking lot during his lunch breaks. Ms. Macchiato tells Rodney not to worry about the ambassador; if they get caught they'll have diplomatic immunity.

On his way into work a couple of days later, Rodney notices a film set in Georgetown and pulls over to check out the production. He approaches a bearded crew member and learns the title of the movie they're filming is *Ignition*.

Rodney: "Ignition?! Where's Thør?"

The professional familiarity throws off the second AD, who looks at Rodney like a deranged civilian instead of the former studio executive responsible for everyone on this set having a job. Rodney decides to return the next day in his barista apron and approaches a production assistant who points out the director to the man from Starbucks. Rodney goes right up to Thør and hands him a Venti Red Eye spiked with Tabasco sauce. The Norwegian takes one sip, grimaces in disgust, and hurls the poisoned cup to the ground.

Rodney: "You're dead, Rosenthal."

The director, a member of the industry assassination league KAOS (Killing as An Organized Sport), can't believe Rodney came all the way to DC to whack him.

Thør: "Who sent you, the janitors?"

(The assassination game pitting studios vs. management companies vs. assistants vs. publicists vs. movie stars vs. agencies coursed through the industry like a California wildfire. The extremist group Justice for Janitors recently claimed responsibility for slitting the throat of literary agent Jerry Makos, significantly upping the stakes for every coffee, lunch, and pitch meeting.)

Rodney explains he's currently VP of cappuccino at the Wisconsin Avenue Starbucks. Thør tells his former *Deathbed* executive to hang out by the video village while he huddles with Roger Deakins. The barista waits about ten minutes before going to work, not caring he would be late this morning.

MONTEZUMA'S REVENGE
Screenplay by Virginia Despres

Sweaty crime piece, chick two-hander, not terrible, Despres spins a period seventies tale about strippers Vicki (vicious sociopath) and Norma Jean (sweet but dumb) who flee a snuff* film set; kill the director who set them up to die in self-defense; carjack a Porsche and hide out at a touristy resort in Ensenada. Vicki and Norma Jean party with vacationing UCLA students Marcus, Bryan, and Karl. Vicki seduces water polo captain Bryan; NFL-bound running back Marcus struggles with explosive diarrhea; Norma Jean falls for aspiring novelist Karl. The vacation turns grisly when Vicki murders Bryan after he catches her going through their suitcases. Karl walks in on Vicki dragging Bryan's corpse and she butchers Karl while Marcus holds his breath in the bathroom. Climactic struggle between BFFs ensues as Norma Jean lops off Vicki's cabeza, dashes for the border and gets shot to death. Marcus only survives because he was on the toilet the whole time. Edgy script makes *Spring Breakers* seem like *Frozen* with its angry attitude, delicious dialogue, and sleazy set-pieces.

snuff

POLICE LINE DO NOT CROSS POLICE LINE DO NOT CROSS POLICE LINE yellow tape cordons off the crime scene of the Wisconsin Avenue Starbucks when Rodney shows up. Questioned and released by DC police, Rodney spends the rest of the day assuring everyone he was not brutally murdered after a local newscaster erroneously names him as one of the coffee baristas found face down on the floor, shot multiple times, with the female manager executed by a single bullet to the head. The next day newly-married Thør Rosenthal and Betsy Yarborough messenger him a shirt: "I Survived the Starbucks Murders and All I Got Was This Lousy T-shirt."

Rodney calls Maeve to say he is alive. Maeve is short with him, on the other line with her husband, explaining why the Secret Service is questioning her whereabouts on the morning of the Starbucks murders and quizzing her about the nature of her relationship with the lone survivor barista. Maeve calls Rodney back and blurts out she was parked outside the Starbucks hoping to see him before his shift started. The ambassador's wife says she didn't hear any gunshots and wonders if the robbers used silencers. Rodney is put off by her stalkerette confession when he is summoned by the Secret Service to explain his connection to an open investigation in Los Angeles involving a prostitute found bludgeoned to death in a backyard Koi pond.

During the interrogation, Secret Service agent Violet Rutledge mentions her screenwriter BFF Stefani Dupin and Rodney says he made an offer to buy her time-traveling serial killer script "Infamous" when he was at Fox but the lit manager Josh Makos sold the spec to MGM. Right then, Violet calls Dupin, who's working on a TV pilot at Intelligentsia Coffee in Silver Lake and puts her BFF on the phone with Rodney. The call is brief and awkward; awkward because the former studio executive is involved with a triple homicide and the screenwriter is very aware of the Koi pond scandal; brief because they have precious little to say other than Rodney admiring her unproduced script and Dupin wishing him luck avoiding life in prison without possibility of parole.

For Rodney and Violet, there is intense mutual curiosity, not to mention sexual attraction, so they make plans to watch Netflix and hang out at Violet's place in Old Town Alexandria. Rodney starts going to Violet's place every night, sending Maeve to voicemail, ignoring the frantic emoji texts declaring her marriage is over; writing her off as too clingy.

Blasting "The Last Day Of Our Acquaintance" on repeat, Maeve tails Rodney leaving Starbucks down Thirty-Fourth Street in her black Range Rover, turning right on M Street, crossing Key Bridge into Roslyn, down Arlington Boulevard, taking George Washington Parkway to Slaters Lane, right on Henry Street, right on Cameron, left on Peyton, clicking off Sinead O'Connor at King Street, where she watches Rodney and Violet making out on the steps of an apartment complex. That night Maeve goes on-line and sends Rodney a T-shirt: "Sorry About What Happens Later."

INFAMOUS
Screenplay by Stefani Dupin

Nifty time-travel thriller delivers the goods on its diabolical plot. Unemployed sanitation worker Leo Wyck chases a serial killer from the future named Sander after he discovers the murderer's personal organizer with sickening holograms of every victim he's left behind. Wyck goes to LA to save Sander's future targets only to fall head over heels for Janine, one of the women whose murder hasn't happened yet. Hapless Wyck gets blamed for the crimes he's trying to prevent since he's always at the scene of the murders. Script stumbles when things get too expository but that's a quibble. Ace plotting escalates the tension in every scene as rising dread envelopes the characters. Electrifying climax delivers as the holograms in the Filofax fade away, the future killings will never happen, and Sander gets jettisoned to the Stone Age. Genre material all the way, but boy, is it well-written.

STARBUCKS SLAYER ADMITS KILLING BARISTAS

GEORGETOWN—Carlos Zamorra told police he shot the manager of a Starbucks because she wouldn't open a safe that contained more than $7,000 in cash. Zamorra, 23, confessed he spent a week planning to rob the Starbucks on Wisconsin Avenue. Police said he demanded the keys, manager Maggie Katz, 27, refused, and he shot her with a .380-caliber pistol. The other baristas were killed after they refused his request for a Mint Chip Frappuccino. Zamorra faces life in prison without parole if he is convicted of the first-degree murder charges. The District of Columbia does not have the death penalty.

TOTAL ECLIPSE OF THE HEART
Screenplay by Lex Sprinkle

Imagine Bonnie Raitt working at a Home Depot by day and singing nightly in a bar band, a heroin-snorting absentee mom to her grown children who live in Canada, a big fat wedding disaster, and you get this funny vehicle for our star/producer client Betsy Yarborough. Sharp script sends rock star mom Lita Dobbs on a vision quest to test her humanity when one daughter's marriage ends and her youngest son Nick is about to have a wedding in Montreal, forcing the golden oldie rocker to confront her dodgy past, her pathetic current situation, and uncertain future. Over the nuptial weekend, shenanigans erupt, culminating with Lita and her band hijacking the wedding to play her favorite cover song, Santana's *Winning*, bringing her broken family on stage for an encore. An actor's piece, everybody in this wedding is well-drawn with Lita's fading star turn most resembling Mickey Rourke in *The Wrestler*. Best line in the script is when an oblivious guest at the rehearsal dinner asks the mother of the groom where she first met Nick and Lita replies, "In the C-Section*."

C-Section

Locking hands to cross P Street, Liam and Anna Muir are struck and killed by a hit and run driver after getting double scoops of ice cream at Thomas Sweet's in Georgetown. With the Vice-President, members of the Foreign Service, friends and family in attendance, Scott Muir gives a moving eulogy about the lifetime they shared, comparing their parents to his favorite Greek myth about Baucis and Philemon, an old married couple who welcomed the Gods into their home as guests when they visited in human form disguised as homeless people. In return, the Gods granted the couple's one wish that when the end came for one of them, the other would die at the same time. When Baucis and Philemon passed away, the Gods turned the couple into trees with branches intertwined so the couple would forever be holding hands. His brother did not speak at the funeral.

Alone at the house in the country overlooking the Potomac River, a grieving Rodney pores through family photo albums, preserved schoolwork papers, Super Bowl souvenir seat cushions from San Diego, Bolletieri tennis camp trophies, library shelves filled with biographies of political figures, countless cookbooks with flour-covered pages, and signed novels authored by Liam and Anna's friends over several decades. In the pages of a Nancy Friday book called *My Mother, My Self*, Rodney stumbles on something completely unexpected: a folded up sonogram of triplets in utero. Their mother had wished loudly and often for a daughter but her production deal shuttered after their delivery at Sibley

Hospital. The sonogram reminds Rodney of a crowded selfie at the Oscars. Heading back to the city, Rodney texts his twin—

Rodney: *you're not gonna believe what I found in the river house*

Scott: *porn?*

Rodney: *sonogram says we were triplets*

Scott: *no way*

Rodney: …

Scott: *where is sis now?*

Rodney: *don't joke*

Scott: *forgotten on birthday I'd be pissed*

Rodney: …

Scott: *google fetus in fetu*

Rodney: *don't call her a teratoma*

Scott: *don't text and drive*

Seeking answers, Rodney treks to Sibley Hospital on MacArthur Boulevard where a wrinkled nurse named Mrs. Green confides to him about an incident at Sibley she witnessed on the day they were born. Working in the OB/GYN ward (her position entailed sweeping after-birth detritus), the nurse glimpsed something slithering around the operating room floor and reported the occurrence to a hospital volunteer whose name she could not recall, a foster caregiver for disadvantaged children. Rodney hires a private investigator and learns the name of the Sibley Hospital volunteer. According to www.findagrave.com, Alma Trout provided mental care for troubled orphans at a foster care home until a suspicious fire destroyed the facility in Silver Spring, Maryland ten years after the Muir triplets were born at Sibley hospital—

Rodney: *I went to her grave*

Scott: *???*

Rodney: *Alma Trout*

Scott: *our sister?*

Rodney: *the orphanage lady who got murdered*

Scott: *you need to get laid*

Rodney: *she's buried next to Zelda and F. Scott Fitzgerald at Old Saint Mary's cemetery*

Scott: *so what*

Rodney: *the expiration date on Alma Trout's headstone matches the date of the orphanage blaze*

Scott: 👏👏👏

NO PLACE LIKE HOME
Screenplay by Michelle Ballo

Reminiscent of *Wrecking Ball*, staggering script offers a tour de force part in Dan Appleby, prestige all the way, fact-based tale of mental illness and homelessness packs a wallop. Told through an early nineties NYC filter where sports columnist Dan sees his homeless parents getting their dinner out of a garbage can, remembering growing up destitute with alcoholic dad Tex, insane mom Josie, and two deranged sisters, a family unit held together with Saran Wrap. Through a series of vivid flashbacks, we see how Tex encouraged Dan to become a writer, how Tex was exploited by his own family members in a child pornography ring, how Dan gets engaged to bank teller Lorna and tells his homeless parents they're not invited to the wedding. There are three breathtaking scenes: one, crashing the engagement party, Tex breaks Dan's nose after losing a thumb wrestling contest; two, Dan says good riddance to a flailing Tex on his deathbed; last scene is a jaw-dropper* when Dan finds out his mother stashed a million dollars in a savings account and they all lived broke for no good reason. Expertly told, the role of batshit crazy Tex is a terrifying daddy not seen since Duvall in *The Great Santini*. Soundtrack of script is Dan's heart breaking.

jaw-dropper

Weeks later, Rodney and Violet get a drink at the Tombs, a rowdy basement bar near Georgetown University when they run into Maeve, of all people, who says she's recently separated from her husband, waiting for her date to show up, and then she joins them in a tight booth near the restrooms against Rodney's futile attempt to get rid of Maeve, who orders several pitchers of Bud Light after her date texts her to say he's parking and will be there any minute. Introductions do not need to be made when Scott arrives at their booth. Violet asks her date if he knows the White House press secretary and Rodney says, "We used to be womb-mates."

Violet and Maeve get along like a house on fire. The conversation shifts to Starbucks. Maeve wonders why is the Secret Service sticking their noses into a Georgetown robbery-homicide? Violet starts spilling details about the execution-style hit (Did you know the Starbucks manager was once a White House intern? Why was there no money taken from the safe?). Maeve asks her date if he has any dirty dishes to add to the pile.

"Somebody reported a DC cop car speeding away from the Starbucks that morning instead of going to the crime scene," says Scott, downing his beer like a rush at Kappa Sig. He adds no one in the neighborhood that morning heard any gunshots, suggesting the killer or killers used silencers; maybe it was the Secret Service behind the assassination, not the other way around.

"Secret Service wearing DC cop uniforms rumor is so last week," scoffs Violet.

"If that girl had just given up the keys to the safe," says Maeve, "they'd all be alive."

"If that girl hadn't been caught bottomless in the Lincoln Bedroom," suggests Scott, "the Secret Service wouldn't have put her on the White House lawn with the First Lady for the Easter egg hunt."

"The Starbucks manager was the President's mistress?" asks Maeve.

"No, the First Lady's."

Rodney excuses himself from the table, eyeing Maeve kissing Scott in full view of Violet, and enters the men's room. From the urinal, he texts his brother—

Rodney: *WTF are you doing?*

Scott: *I saw her first*

Rodney: *full metal straitjacket*

Scott: …

Rodney: *ask your date why she was at Starbucks that morning*

Scott: *This is Maeve. I'm using your brother's phone. Party at Violet's.*

Rodney: *go ahead without me*

Scott: 😎 😎 😎

FUCKINGHAM PALACE
Screenplay by Tabitha Von Swine

Sexy sixteenth century period piece serves up eviscerating conversations, tantric set-pieces, and sumptuous costumes. While not explicit, sexually charged lesbian chamber drama brings the heat. Lording over everyone in court, Anne Boleyn fails to please her royal husband Henry VIII (struggling with gout) while Anne's lascivious lover Priscilla (the bride of Sir Thomas More) whispers in the King's ear about the threat of Prussia. Henry VIII is hilarious, a walking hard-on with an insatiable appetite for mutton. Then, a new rival for Anne's affection emerges: the omnisexual maid Abigail, who instigates bedroom wars that threaten the crown. Anne seals her doom taking on Abigail, a trollop with viper's instincts who heals Henry's gout, massages his legs (and more), poisons Priscilla, and convinces Henry VIII to chop off the Queen's head. It ends very badly for Abigail, who's banished to a slimy Paris brothel. Tantalizing material. Worthy of top talent. A royal romp*.

royal romp

Tearing open a MAGNUM™ wrapper with her teeth, "That's quite a scar you've got," says Maeve in Old Town Alexandria, naked, pressing her jagged birthmark against Scott's identical wound, resembling conjoined twins Chang and Eng (one died in his sleep, the other woke up to a corpse and died of fright). "Yours is gnarlier," says Rodney, guzzling South African Merlot, swallowing a Quaalude, thinking over and over about Alma Trout's expiration date on her tombstone; Maeve turning over, catching Rodney and Scott bumping fists, "You guys did not just do that!" Rodney imagining Secret Service agents executing terrified baristas with silencers; flash and it's Maeve driving away from Thomas Sweet after running over their parents; Violet joining the cluster, snorting banana coke, kissing the ex-wife of the Irish Ambassador, pulling her away from the brothers; flash and it's Maeve executing everybody inside the Starbucks except Rodney, late for work; Maeve tonguing Violet, Rodney throbbing, Violet ejaculating, Maeve urging Scott to step up to her mouth; Scott thrusting, Maeve choking, natal scar so unnerving Rodney goes soft.

BRAINIAC
Screenplay by Bima Stander

Cerebral, oddly affecting drama about a small town farmer afflicted with a brain tumor that renders him super smart. Melvin O'Malley takes his small town by storm when word of his phenomenal gift gets out (it's rumored he was abducted and probed by aliens). Melvin uses his new powers to learn foreign languages, farm gigantic tomatoes, and along the way, charm the pants off of sexy widow Jayma and become a father figure to her two teenage daughters. Character-driven fantasy proposes that everyone has this wondrous ability if only we could unlock the source in our minds. Dazzling writing handles the science fiction as distinctively as the relationships. Script offers a real connection between Melvin and Jayma, brainy conversations, and the town's gossipy neighbors are a hoot. Villains of the piece are reptilian government suits who want to capture Melvin (think *E.T.*) so they can militarize his telekinesis. Tragic third act goes for the hankies with Melvin's sad passing from the brain tumor, reminding us how fleeting life can be.

STARBUCKS SLAYER
SUSPECT RECANTS

RUMORS CONTINUE TO CIRCULATE ABOUT ROSE
GARDEN ACTIVITES AND INTERN.

"I swear on my daughter's grave I didn't do this,"
Carlos Zamorra told the judge in the case after
police said he admitted killing ex-White House
intern **Maggie Katz** and two other employees
during a botched stickup. The triple murders
have raised troubling questions for the White
House. Why was former Oval Office staffer
Katz shot execution-style with a bullet to the
back of her head? If the motive was robbery,
why was no money taken from the safe? At
Camp David, a reporter asked, "Mr. President,
did you cry for Maggie Katz?"

IGNITION*
Revisions by Manuel Orantes

Explosive romantic actioner with dynamite characters elevates this enthralling tale of a mad bomber who takes on a fearless DEA agent and a wheelchair-bound bomb expert during July Fourth festivities in the nation's capital. Federal agent Lacey Tornado captures drug kingpin Rico Sangre and brings him to DC where he is sentenced to death for his crimes. Former bomb squad expert Harvey Cross, confined to a wheelchair, is brought into the mix when his turncoat colleague Grimes starts a bombing campaign throughout the city to force Sangre's release. Tornado and Cross form an unlikely alliance, fall in love, and send the mad bomber to Hades. Compelling at every turn, character-driven script offers a white-knuckle ride with an unexpected romance bubbling to the surface. For Antwon Legion, Cross is quite an intriguing lead (charming, daring, yet paralyzed). Similarly, well-drawn Lacey Tornado is a rose with thorns (sharp-tongued with glimpses of tenderness under her Kevlar vest). Tightly scripted, IGNITION moves like a lit fuse, and the romance that develops is tested at every turn; these two flirt even when a bomb could go off in their faces (banter is great). Final third at the Washington Monument is action-packed and ends with a kiss, not a bang.

Ignition

"I may be paralyzed, but I still have to frisk you," says Legion.

"Knock it off Antwon," says Rodney, "Violet's with the Secret Service."

"Agents: with 'em, without 'em, can't live."

Shrieking seagulls, walkie-talkies squawking, Teamsters humping cables as the star of *Ignition* greets Rodney and his date at the briny Southwest Waterfront marina. Violet can't stop staring at Legion, goateed, movie star handsome, playing the paralyzed explosives expert—

"Antwon, it's me."

Legion: "How many guesses do I get?"

"Let me give you a hint: Battery Place."

Legion: "Battery Place?"

"Don't tell me you forgot what street you grew up on?"

Legion: "I grew up on a lot of streets."

"Come on Antwon, think real hard."

Legion: "Give me another clue."

"Alma Trout."

Breaking character, Legion leaps out of the wheelchair: "My sister from another mister!"

"Look at you, Oscar winner."

Legion: "Look at you, protecting the President."

Rodney: "You two went to prom?"

"Hell no, Antwon and I grew up in the same foster home."

Rodney: "Foster home?"

Legion: "Remember when you deep fried that Trout—"

Violet shushes the movie star with a middle finger to her lips. The second AD interrupts to declare Harvey Cross is needed on set. Legion falls into his wheelchair and motors away to save the nation's capital from a mad bomber.

"Silver Spring," grasps Rodney.

"Hey, how'd you know that?" asks Violet.

The ex-studio executive turns away from his sister, the one not named Maeve, hot bile waving hello to his esophagus, and swallows the acidic gob of realization in his throat.

WHEELIE
Screenplay by Ed Hider

Familiar dramatic territory a la *The Waterdance*, but this remains a devastating ride. Wheelchair-bound from a freak ping pong accident, Don Abramson is a functional drug addict searching for his birth mother who can draw better than Picasso. Don undergoes nightmarish surgeries, suicidal thoughts, and alcoholic benders until he quits boozing and takes control of his life. Don's work as a political cartoonist takes off during Obama's Presidential campaign, which brings him mad fame and a national platform. Unconventional structure, witty title cards, and quick flashbacks all play beautifully. Don's imagination runs wild through animated sequences yet script stays grounded with an off-beat romance for Don with waitress Molly, who overcomes her own scars (scalded as an infant by a spilt cup* of hot McDonald's coffee). Don's cartoons attacking Sarah Palin are hilarious, but when Don meets Barack Obama in the restroom at Molly's diner, it's the candidate at the urinal who laughs the loudest. Don never does locate his birth mother, but Molly finds him in script's final triumph. Only a first draft, we should get into this for casting and support this miraculous wheelie.

spilt cup

Rodney: *where the fuck r U?*

Scott: *Brady press room briefing in 15 wassup*

Rodney: *Violet mad at me for going through her things*

Scott: *underwear?*

Rodney: *looking for police uniform*

Scott: *yer insane you think she did Starbucks?*

Rodney: *our sister was there that morning*

Scott: …

Rodney: *remember Alma Trout?*

Scott: *5th grade, first kiss?*

Rodney: *the lady I told you about*

Scott: *which one big tits or gap between her teeth?*

Rodney: *Violet burned down foster home not Maeve*

Scott:

Rodney: *we're next*

Scott: *sounds like Thør movie*

Rodney: *shut up*

Scott: *novel?*

Rodney: *Violet killed mom and dad*

Scott: *and the Kennedys*

Rodney: *be serious*

Scott: *I can't have this convo about mom and dad you're upsetting me*

Rodney: *OK*

Scott: *no word from Maeve since menage*

Rodney: *thought she liked you*

Scott: *not me she liked*

Rodney: *wish you would pick up phone*

Scott: *wish you would go to rehab*

DIE HARDEST
Screenplay by Jeb Ferguson

Geriatric final installment of the anti-terrorist franchise gives John McClane the *Gran Torino* treatment with spectacular results. A fictionalized version of the Mumbai attack at the Taj Mahal hotel by Pakistani gunmen, retired cop McClane happens to be attending his grand-daughter's wedding when jihadists take over the palatial hotel. Instead of demanding a ransom, the terrorists go room by room executing tourists, prostitutes, and maids with machine guns. Packed with action sequences, if there's one guy you want to take on these murdering jihadists, it's John McClane. Conflicted terrorist Ayman surrenders midway through the attack and joins the geriatric action hero to end the massacre, ultimately taking a bullet meant for McClane. The hotel guests are saved, the Indian military ends the siege, but alas, on the plane ride home, our gun-toting grandpa expires in his sleep. Let's hope the test audience cards demand a new ending and John McClane doesn't die hard*.

die hard

Selling the country house was emotional to say the least for the Muir brothers. Leaning on the white metal fence overlooking the Potomac River, Rodney stares for the last time at the family of Ospreys skimming the body of water outside the empty crib, a transcendent view that now belonged to NBA draft bust Methusaleh Dandridge (recently traded to the Wizards in exchange for cash, Memphis center Jamarcus Green, and power forward Li Jeng). Rodney blinks, unexpectedly sees a vision of Century City skyscrapers, magenta sun reflected off the glass skyline, where did that sudden yearning come from? Then, a text arrives—

Scott: *going to Georgetown Starbucks*

Rodney: *murder Bux is closed*

Scott: *Violet wants to tell me something*

Rodney: *what?*

Scott: …

Rodney: *pregnant?*

Scott: …

Rodney: *just tried calling you*

Scott: …

No text arrives. Rodney jumps into his car and heads for the Starbucks in Georgetown. Old Fort Road to Allentown Road.

Right on 210 Indian Head Highway. Rodney slows down for the speed trap at Malcolm X Boulevard. Calls his brother again. Gets voicemail. Exits the ramp to 295 North.

Steering toward Washington, cellphone chirping, Rodney takes the call from an agency assistant at Omniscience/Ragnarök: "Please hold for Lester Barnes and Walter Nikolovski."

Nikolovski: "Hey, it's Walter. I thought you were dead."

Rodney: "Stop reading coverage."

Lester: "What's new with Jew, Rodney?"

Rodney: "That's a loaded question."

Left onto I-695 for a minute, Rodney turns onto Southwest Freeway, past the Capitol building, veering over three lanes to get off at Maine Avenue, reminding him of Highland and the 101 North and the five lanes it takes to cross over to Barham Avenue—

Lester: "Nikolovski and I were talking about you at the celebration of life for Arthur Livingstone, such great creative instincts, we were wondering, have you ever considered being an agent?"

Independence Avenue to Ohio Drive, Whitehurst Freeway to K Street, Rodney says he can't talk, he's racing to save his brother from being murdered by their triplet sister who went insane in utero, tossed onto the operating room floor by careless doctors, a subcutaneous mass of hair, teeth, and eyeballs rescued by a hospital—

Lester: "So dark, I love it. Walter, get Screen Gems on the phone. Call it *Sin Utero*. Who else has heard this pitch?"

Right on Twenty-Ninth Street, left onto Q Street, right on Wisconsin Avenue, Rodney keeps ranting about the volunteer nurse who raised the imp only to die in a mysterious fire, their vanished triplet growing up to exact revenge, running over their elderly parents, seducing the brothers at her place in Alexandria, this is not a pitch, this is real, shouts Rodney, he has to get to Starbucks—

"Seek help," says Lester Barnes, hanging up, regretting the call.

On Wisconsin, Rodney finds a space, hops out of his car, and sprints toward the ambush. Turning left on Thirty-Fourth Street, green Starbucks awning now visible, he arrives at the coffee house parking lot, and barges into—

A candlelight vigil for Maggie Katz.

Rodney searches for his brother among the faces of DC Statehood advocates, political mosquitos, homeless dudes sipping coffee, and butch members of the Bethesda Lesbian Avengers singing "Happy Birthday" for their fallen barista at this anti-violence observance/birthday celebration.

Flash of Maeve among the lesbians; flame hair shorn off like an army grunt or cancer patient, unclear which team drafted her; glimpse of Scott in the carnival-esque parking lot; Rodney runs past a fire-eating demonstration to save his brother when an unsmiling Violet enters the frame—

Targeting her like a drone strike, Violet finds Maeve, planting a soulful kiss on her lips, tongue sliding around her girlfriend's eager mouth, leaving the Muir brothers staring at the Sapphic couple.

Scott: "Well, that explains that."

Rodney: "Violet didn't do Starbucks."

Scott: "T'was beauty she wanted."

Rodney: "I can think of a worse ending."

FRED 62
Screenplay by Pat Hobby

Lame LA noir/tame pastiche of *Kiss Kiss Bang Bang* paints a moody portrait of Los Angeles dripping with cocaine, murderous goons, hot dames, and a silver Ferrari Testarossa Spider racing the streets of the big nipple*, signifying nothing; a total bore. Hipster and local "fixer" Fred 62 can get rid of any problem; anything you need, Fred 62 can wiggle it for you. A chiseled lead who talks his way out of every jam, Fred 62 is tasked by mysterious Korean businessman Ike to find his missing daughter Julia just as he's about to purchase the LA hockey team (Ike is buying the NHL franchise to launder his illicit profits). Fred 62 rescues Julia from her Yakuza kidnappers, survives a plane crash, turns Ike over to the Feds, and moves to Miami without Julia, who pours herself a glass of Drano rather than return to a life looking over her shoulder. For Antwon Legion, the prose is slick, edgy but not really, Shiite script, a talkfest that goes nowhere fast.

the big nipple

Michael Tolkin introduces the author of the hour at a 7:00 p.m. SRO crowd at Book Soup on Sunset Boulevard:

"How many studio executives does it take to screw in a lightbulb?"

(*wait*)

"Does it have to be a lightbulb?"

(*laughter*)

"Most of us here knew Rodney when he was a weasel at Paramount, Twentieth Century Fox, and some criminal outfit called Bellerophon, where he oversaw production of sixteen motion pictures. Those guys stiffed me for that polish I did on *Plasma Sluts*."

(*laughter*)

"*Entertainment Weekly* described his debut novel *Sin Utero* as '*House of Cards* meets Stephen King.' Please welcome an exciting new voice, Rodney Muir!"

(*applause*)

At the podium with a microphone, the novelist addresses the packed house: "Thank you Book Soup for having us. Thank you, Tyson Cornell, for publishing me. Seeing all of you here tonight under one roof reminds me of my first wedding."

(*laughter*)

"Hopefully you'll read the book and not the coverage."

(*laughter*)

"This is from my first novel *Sin Utero*."

(*silence*)

"'Not good—thought the suicide bomber as he tried unsuccessfully to catch a cab on La Cienega, waving his arms and shouting "Taxi" to indifferent and off-duty drivers who sped past him. Clinking down Olympic, the eighty pounds of nails and screws and metal shrapnel he had purchased at Home Depot made walking almost impossible and his vest was starting to itch. Raising a hand to shield his eyes from the sun's harsh rays, a yellow LA Taxi pulled over and he climbed into the backseat, holding his bellybomb, appearing more like a pregnant man than a martyr who intended to destroy the forces of evil that had already occupied Beverly Hills, Brentwood, Laurel Canyon, parts of Beachwood, and Malibu Colony. The cab driver, Palestinian, first name, Yousef, recently diagnosed with Pancreatic Cancer, would eventually die in a Cairo dungeon after his rendition did not produce the information desired by the State Department. As Yousef picked up his clipboard, the passenger in the back seat coughed ostentatiously to cover the sound of the Glad bags sloshing with Hexamine, H2H2, sugar, and Citric Acid C6H8O7. For an instant, the passenger feared he would prematurely expostulate. A silence filled the taxicab as they hit traffic on Olympic heading toward Century City and the end of the passenger's life. The suicide bomber powered down his window to feel the sun on his forehead as the taxicab rode up the Avenue of the Stars ramp and arrived at Nakatomi Plaza, where valet parking attendants opened his door. Alone in the elevator, he looked at his reflection in the mirrored ceiling until the doors opened, revealing a posse of unsmiling agents waiting for the janitor to emerge from the lift and release the IED—'"

Later, during the Q & A with the audience: "As a studio executive, you developed hundreds of scripts and passed on thousands, did you always want to be a writer?"

Rodney: "I think I was born to write this book."

"Congratulations on *Sin Utero*. I chased the rights after I read the galley."

Rodney: "Thank you, where do you work?"

"I work at Hulu. My question is: when you were writing this loosely autobiographical novel about the Starbucks murders, did you ever think if *Sin Utero* became a best seller, your psychotic triplet sister might show up at the launch party? Maybe she's here tonight. Maybe you'll sign her copy."

Rodney: "That's your novel."

(*laughter*)

"You have a blurb from the biggest movie star in the world. What's Legion really like?"

Rodney: "Antwon's the best. We first met when his agent Lester Barnes called me to suggest Antwon for the role of the psychiatrist in *Faith Don't Leave*. I took Antwon to dinner at Roscoe's Chicken and Waffles and I left the table convinced he was the shrink."

"Were you on set when Justice for Janitors gunned down the writers and the craft service guy?"

Rodney: "No, but I went to the 'Faith Who Left' memorial at Hollywood Forever. I overheard these assistants talking about the funeral and one of the assistants asked the other if she knew the victims and the assistant said she didn't know anyone. 'Then why did you go?' And the assistant said, 'Are you kidding? I went for the contacts.'"

STARBUCKS ROBBER PLEADS GUILTY TO AVOID EXECUTION

SENTENCING ENDS PUBLIC SPECULATION OF 'ORAL OFFICE' CONNECTION TO WHITE HOUSE

CAPITOL HILL—Carlos Zamorra confessed yesterday he killed three Starbucks employees during an ill-fated robbery attempt. "Yes sir, I shot them," Zamorra told the crowded courtroom before Judge Derek Cooper sentenced him to life in prison without the possibility of parole. No reason was given why the White House sought the death penalty over the objections of DC prosecutors in this particular case. As part of the plea bargain, prosecutors agreed not to charge his grandmother with lesser crimes. Zamorra wept as bailiffs led him away in chains.

WHOREGASM

OMNISCIENCE/RAGNARÖK
SCRIPT BURNING RAISES IRE

The bonfire of screenplays outside powerhouse **Omniscience/Ragnarök** sparked a conflagration of protests between writers and religious leaders and LAPD officers protecting agent trainees dumping armloads of scripts into a pyre of ceremonial flames. The summer solstice event presided over by honcho **Lester Barnes** was celebrated as a "condemnation of studio culture."

LEGION   WEINTRAUB

Oscar winner **Antwon Legion**, attending the event in support of his agency's efforts, declined to comment. A budding archeologist, Legion unearthed his ancestral crypt last week in Iraq and found the bones of several jackals. Spotted among the protesters was Jewish Defense League's **Meir Weintraub**, who reminded the agency underlings: "Where they burn scripts, so, too, will they in the end burn human beings."

SPACE INVADER
Screenplay by Chip Ganem

Think *Alien*. Think *Gravity*. Now stop thinking. Imagine a contained genre script set on a space station after the discovery of life on Venus. Imagine a single cell escaping a microscope and consuming everybody on board. The real star of this show, nicknamed Marge, is the carnivorous amoeba, not the scaredy-cat astronauts trying to avoid getting eaten. Two possible roles here for Antwon Legion: Lt. Pippen, the sole survivor of this space ordeal who unknowingly escorts Marge in his escape pod to complete her buffet of humanity on Earth, or the more interesting part of cyborg astronaut Owen, who gives up the ghost in a death match with Marge near the halfway mark. Director did *Stockholm Chill*. Not familiar with his work. Not enough character beats for the other astronauts to shine. Not enough memorable lines. Script desperately needs more trailer moments. On the flip side, Marge could find fame as an iconic boogeyman* in this space opera about life on Venus ending life on Earth.

boogeyman

"The real Anti-Christ is he who turns the wine of an original idea into the water of mediocrity."

—Eric Hoffer

FALLING SNOW
Screenplay by Michelle LaVey

Intimate tale with powerful imagery, an existential character journey, set largely in snow-drenched Montana. For Betsy Yarborough, lead Yetta is on every page and almost every frame investigating the mystery of her life: *Who was my mother? Who was my father? Who am I?* Told through a series of stunning events, Yetta works at Whole Foods in San Francisco when her grandmother dies and she inherits the family farm in Montana. Yetta confronts her estranged father in prison, a serial rapist who murdered her college roommate, and the convict tells Yetta she was adopted. An embarrassing one-night stand with a rancher in Kalispell leads to an unplanned pregnancy* she debates keeping but decides to abort. Yetta regrets that decision, settles into her ranch, learns how to raise cattle and aims to start all over. Powerful last scene has Yetta at a nursing home where her Alzheimer's-afflicted birth mother first mistakes Yetta for her nurse, then starts calling Yetta her daughter, unaware this stranger actually is the child she once gave up for adoption. Truly compelling character-driven female quest movie is worth considering, a star vehicle about a stranger in a strange land.

unplanned pregnancy

Libra Livingstone spent her whole life praying for her dad to die. Arthur Livingstone spent weeks praying for her abortion. Libra's mother Yalda Frazee chucked a career as a top TV packaging agent at Omniscience to raise her love child in the Hollywood Hills with the head of motion picture talent who never gave his kid so much as a hug. Famished for affection, she maintained her size zero by taking up long-distance running along with years of bulimic purging. When her boobs got too big and Libra was taken out of high school for breast-reduction surgery, she remembered her dad calling her "selfish, selfish, selfish."

As an agent trainee at Omniscience/Ragnarök right out of Bennington, Libra lied to everyone about her last name, no one, not even the janitors, knew she was Arthur Livingstone's kid. Libra dressed conservatively, never wore makeup, and enjoyed her anonymity as she rolled calls, floated on desks, and sorted envelopes in the mailroom. Interested in writing script coverage, Libra started making out with Larry Mersault at lunchtime in his office, which led to quickies on his couch while everyone attended the Wednesday morning staff meeting.

(Late at the office, a janitor walked in on them 69-ing: Libra, lapping away, oblivious; tortuous orgasm flooding out of him; office door closing; Mersault glimpsing the janitor's warty tail, no earlobes, not of this area code, a day player from a Thør Rosenthal movie.)

Arthur Livingstone learned of their relationship and arranged for Libra to get a job elsewhere as a reader at Bellerophon Pictures, where she could pick up scripts, learn the ins and outs of the business, and avoid bringing shame onto the agency. When Benny Pantera invited the new girl to his latest production, *Plasma Sluts*, Libra had no idea the set visit would be the first time she did it for money. At a derelict warehouse in North Hollywood, Thør Rosenthal was so smitten with his ravishing visitor he cast Libra on the spot as a murdered hooker retrieved from a trash dumpster by a madman plastic surgeon utilizing body parts for his own twisted ambition. Libra refused to have her throat slit for free. Benny Pantera suggested she should jump into the makeup trailer for a hundred bucks before she jumped into the trash container; Libra haggled for five hundred; three Benjamins later, she was topless, covered in garbage, and ready for her close up.

JITTERS
Screenplay by P.T. Sparks

Dark romantic comedy apes *Pretty Woman* without the humor, charm, and universal appeal. Unpleasant characters, bitchy dialogue, yet a tight structure keep things moving. Implausible tale has aspiring restauranteur Oscar falling for a black stripper on the eve of his loveless marriage to Sophia. Put on a subway train unconscious, wearing a ball gag, black leggings, and dressed in a negligee by his groomsmen, Oscar wakes up (no wallet, no memory how he got there) in a Bronx pigsty with the bachelor party stripper Rwanda, a heroin-addicted prostitute who agrees to help him get to his wedding for three thousand* bucks. After enduring a string of grim ordeals to get to the Plaza Hotel, instead of saying "I do" at the altar, Oscar follows his dream to open up a restaurant in California with Rwanda at his side. Premise of a guy falling for his bachelor party stripper is given an unexpectedly gritty flavor. However, the writing doesn't sparkle and the story is mostly a flat line. Low point of the tale is when Rwanda prostitutes herself to pay for their plane tickets; at the wedding, she meets Oscar's lecherous father-in-law and it turns out he's the john who hired her. Call this one *Runaway Groom*.

three thousand

Three Thousand by J. F. Lawton was originally developed at now-defunct Vestron Pictures by cult filmmaker Donald Cammell (1934–1996) as a stark drama about a cocaine-addled streetwalker who gets paid $3,000 by a businessman to be his escort for a week. Disney acquired the script, called it *Pretty Woman*, hired Barbara Benedek to do a page one rewrite, and cast Julia Roberts as the most beloved whore of all time.

EFFERVESSENCE
Screenplay by Guido Valentin

Beautiful, sexy, fractured tale of amour, more high-brow euro art film than anything else. Actors and audiences will likely be reminded of *The English Patient*. Gripping romance between Sugar, an ex-model turned clam diver who risks her life on a commercial fishing boat, and new boyfriend Charlie, handsome Brooklynite, an "oil consultant" held hostage by ISIS militants in Kurdistan, near death, unable to communicate with Sugar, who's caught in a terrible storm that threatens to drown everyone on board. Engaging script has the two lovers dreaming of their first meeting at a motel in sweltering Abilene, Texas, followed by kinky sessions in bed; Sugar finds her true calling under the sea; ex-Mafia hitman Charlie joins the CIA to fight jihadists and ends up in captivity. Sugar survives her catastrophe but Charlie isn't so lucky (it's unclear if his rescuers arrive in time to save him). Last scene finds the two of them 69-ing* back in Abilene, hinting this might be Charlie's final thought, or, more hopefully, a flash-forward to their reunion in the not-too-distant future. Best script so far this year.

69-ing

"Get dressed. We have to check out by noon."

"You got pretty wasted at the premiere last night," says a butt-naked Libra, lounging on her belly in bed, surrounded by Four Seasons pillows, half-watching the surgical procedure butchering the star of MY 800 POUND LIFE on television.

"How was *Effervescence*? I don't remember any of it," says Rodney, looking for his socks under the California King.

"Why did you hire the guy who directed *Stockholm Chill*? The script was so much better."

"Benny owed a favor to Lester—what's wrong? Did I say 'I love you' again? I'm sorry."

"Could you help me make rent this month? My dad's not supporting me anymore."

"Your dad's a pretty big deal in this town—"

"You're either with the terrorists or against them."

"What are we talking about?"

"I need two grand," says Libra, biting her lower lip.

"Will you take a check?"

"Cash is safer."

"ATM limit is three hundred," says Rodney.

"Can you go into the bank today, please? Otherwise, I'm clucking in the henhouse."

"I'll give you the dough tonight at Hama."

"Thanks, boss."

BAD GRANDMA
Screenplay by Danny Dortmund

Not the sweetest romantic comedy, BAD GRANDMA crackles with blunt language, blunt sexual situations, blunt characters talking about HPV, how to be rude to a clitoris, the friend zone, low self-esteem, and love/sex addiction. There's an off-putting story here about Jake, a womanizer who cherishes his best friend's grandmother who took his virginity in college. That grandmother Elaine has her own infatuation with a married obstetrician who's been sleeping with her for thirty years because she's still the best lay he's ever had. When Jake and Elaine reconnect later in S.F. she's planning her funeral and he's worth millions after selling his company to Microsoft. When Elaine doesn't wake up after a night of marathon sex, Jake realizes she was "the one" at her funeral. Script references *Misery* and *Pretty Woman* for a reason; fairy tales set in San Francisco where women cry at the opera sometimes end badly. Awkward script has explicit scenes of fisting, masturbation, and "romantic" kisses with your best friend's grandmother. Audience may be limited.

THINK STRAIGHT
Pilot by Charlotte Jensen

Compelling pilot establishes an intriguing character you want to follow but suffers slightly from rich white people disease. Lesbian therapist Janet loves her oncologist husband Paula, adores their young daughter Chloe, and enjoys a thriving shrink practice in Manhattan. After listening to patient Melissa complaining about her selfish ex-BF Jeremy and their matching π tattoos (she thinks 3.1415926 looks dumb on her neck yet cool on Jeremy), Janet becomes infatuated with a singer-songwriter at her coffee shop who flirts with her, she calls herself "Lola," and the nameless guy invites her to his show. Janet suspects Paula's new secretary Val is trouble and she's right, with Val going down on Paula in the office elevator. Janet lies to Paula and journeys to the nightclub as "Lola" to hang out with the singer who turns out to have a π tattoo (!) on his neck. Their flirtation leads to an unprotected quickie in a bathroom stall and the pilot ends with Janet uncertain about her marriage, uncertain about Jeremy, and uncertain about her sexuality. As a series for Betsy Yarborough, think Mary Tyler Moore on steroids; a therapist in need of a therapist; plenty of uncharted psychological territory to explore week in, week out, through this compelling pursuit of a double life*.

double life

Libra liked the idea of walking into Saks Fifth Avenue in Beverly Hills, counting nineteen crisp hundred dollar bills, and zipping out with the royal blue leather Yves St. Laurent satchel purse she always coveted but never could afford. This particular handbag was not paid for by her sugar boss Rodney Muir, who was affectionate but sometimes stingy, which annoyed Libra greatly; certainly not from Lester Barnes, happy to give his sugar daughter a little something extra for the road, which made up for those nipple clamps she abhorred; the cheddar was not from Walter Nikolovski, whom Arthur Livingstone had ostensibly arranged for Libra to strategize about a CE gig at Paramount but instead they got a suite across the street at the Park Hyatt (she charged him triple for their clumsy hour and a half, waiting outside Wells Fargo for the sugar llama to hand over stacks of banded twenties). In truth, it was new regular Dollars Muttlan, (flavor-of-the-month screenwriter turned industry leper after *Warlords of Arkadia* bombed) who booked her every Friday night in August for a porn star experience at twenty-five hundred a pop after a midnight show at the New Beverly where they watched TRUE ROMANCE, THE LAST WAVE, NUDE NUDES, and THE 4TH MAN, ending up at Swingers in the Beverly Laurel Motor Inn, bemoaning the business over strawberry milkshakes and sweet potato fries with ranch dressing, checking into the "romance room" upstairs where Dollars would occasionally make Libra come.

TRUE FIBS
Screenplay by Bud Wiggins

Explosive actioner cares about its characters while delivering the carnage. On the trail of nuclear terrorists, CIA agent Jerry Trasker realizes his family is hopelessly dysfunctional because he's been lying for years about his true profession to unhappy wife Lisa and college-bound daughter Skylar. When Jerry learns she is contemplating an affair with a "real 007" who's a lying shoe salesman, he tells Lisa the truth about his actual occupation. A skeptical Lisa still doesn't believe her husband when terrorists kidnap them and Jerry shows off his action hero chops and saves the world from Armageddon. There's a nice subtext about deception that's subtly woven into the narrative fabric. That Wiggins pulls off this feisty spy-family concept with such an affecting delivery is fucking remarkable. For Hugo Slater, relationship-driven script adds unexpected dramatic layers to its hi-octane set-pieces and memorably presents a dysfunctional family healing itself.

BILLBOARD BACKLASH

OFFENSIVE POSTERS REMOVED AFTER RESIDENTS PROTEST 'TORTURE PORN' CAMPAIGN

Hung over from a bachelor party thrown by CEO Benny Pantera, execs at Bellerophon Pictures arrived at work yesterday to find their voicemails full with messages from teachers, feminists, and community leaders voicing outrage over the revolting ads blanketing the city.

A spokesperson for Bellerophon admitted the disturbing billboards had gone up without MPAA approval but said in a statement the images were sent "in error" to an outside advertising company and dismissed allegations the company knew the controversy would raise awareness for the horror pic.

"Plasma Sluts," directed by Thør Rosenthal and starring Betsy Yarborough as a helicopter mom held captive by a mad Beverly Hills plastic surgeon, opens Friday.

WHORE ON THE RANGE
Screenplay by Sherry Naing

Starkly compelling script about the wages of sin* through the lens of Lacy Keller, a self-employed writer going through a divorce, raising three girls on a small farm, can't afford Christmas presents, can't afford much of anything, fights with her bitter ex-husband over custody, faces foreclosure, hints of a lesbian romance with babysitter Perry, turns tricks in her basement, sells her livestock, converts her barn into a brothel, loses her kids in a custody battle, and recruits other mothers to join her prostitution empire. As a divorced ex-waitress and aspiring hog farmer Lacy discovers she excels at one thing: whoring herself out. Depressing ending has Lacy dreaming of selling her life story to Hollywood, attending the LA premiere, walking the red carpet when she wakes up, back to reality, selling her body to a migrant worker. For Betsy Yarborough, grim tale of an underdog hooker with her bootstraps in the air might not be prestige. Writer-director was at Sundance years ago with a similarly subtle woman's picture called *On The Rag.*

wages of sin

Dental records identified Libra Livingstone as the murdered prostitute at the bottom of the Koi pond in the Bel Air residence owned by Benny Pantera; her father had no idea she was on IMDB.

5 DAYS/6 NIGHTS
Screenplay by Isaac Mazzola

Manipulative piece of romantic fluff fails to pull off its *Castaway* concept, needs a rewrite more than a life preserver. *UTERUS* magazine publisher/militant feminist Janine Roth dumps her self-absorbed tennis pro beau only to be trapped in the Caribbean with cocky pilot Freddy Galdiaz after their propeller plane crash lands on an uninhabited island. Predictable sparks and character-history conversations follow, with the pair constantly arguing, reluctantly copulating, trapped in the blue lagoon until their rescue, and return to the deserted isle a year later for their shotgun wedding. Dialogue is unspeakable. Worst scene is when Freddy and Janine read aloud and answer highly personal questions from her own magazine's *Cosmo*-type sex questionnaire. Not funny*. Maybe if these two idiots were given a volleyball or some clever lines, we might want to watch them fish, fight, and figure out a way off this island. Think of the violence of *Swept Away*, picture Phyllis Diller and Don Rickles stranded together, and you get the idea of this irritating script.

Not funny

Arthur Livingstone, the object of a citywide manhunt, attends the *5 Days/6 Nights* premiere in Westwood after killing his daughter Libra, a good-time girl whose client list astounds the industry. Fleeing the after-party, Livingstone carjacks a Range Rover on Wilshire, leads police and news helicopters on a televised freeway chase until the octogenarian runs out of gas, slits his throat, and finger paints in blood ƧƎ⅃Иᴖᴙ ИOIᴖƎ⅃ on the windshield.

WRECKING BALL
Screenplay by Yancy Drapkin

Prestige material resonates on a character level of *American Beauty, Good Will Hunting,* and *Ordinary People*. Moving script about a widow named Mavis who loses her husband in a senseless lawnmower accident and trashes her corporate law career, destroys her relationships with toxic friends, and finally, symbolizing her state of mind, bulldozes her house in suburbia with the help of an eager Mexican wrecking crew. *Monsters Ball* was like this script, ferociously well-drawn, exploring grief and shattered lives through a completely character-driven love story with flashes of unbearable drama. When Mavis meets a pot-smoking widower struggling to raise a son who's a bully, she schools the boy on how to make a chocolate mousse and shows the widower how to be a better father. Turns out our one woman wrecking ball kept her terminal cancer diagnosis hidden from everybody and her late husband never told Mavis about his second family outside their marriage. Life is tough, life is weird, life is short, script seems to say, so figure it out before your number is up.

RETAIL THERAPY FOR TEN-PERCENTERY

ARE AGENTS AND NUKES TWO GREAT TASTES THAT TASTE GREAT TOGETHER?

Omniscience/Ragnarök has been on a roll since the marquee signing of Antwon Legion, purchasing biotech giant **AmZyne**, Los Alamos-based arms manufacturer **Tregaron Enterprises**, and **Demeter**, a multi-national agro-chemical company specializing in genetically engineered seed.

"The global reach of these opportunities provide a strong, strategic stockpile to our growing portfolio," said a spokesperson for Omniscience/Ragnarök **(NASDAQ: OMRA)**, the global leader in entertainment, sports, agriculture, pharmaceuticals, fashion, and military technologies.

What is their ultimate goal? Is it to create a geopolitical disruptor-entertainment influencer that represents the talent, feeds the hungry, buys advertising agencies to promote their clients at Omniscience/Ragnarök-owned sporting events, sells weapons around the world to the highest bidder, and produces original content through mobile apps invented by their own tech start-ups to create a company bigger than Apple?

"We want Putin to return our calls," said Hollywood super-agent Lester Barnes from an undisclosed location.

GEEZER
Screenplay by Franklin Brauner

Ludicrous but accessible comic book hero with global appeal could be a franchise actioner for Hugo Slater or Antwon Legion. Two-thousand-year-old Moe Reilly is half *Highlander*, half *Deadpool*. Tone is *Sin City*; action is over-the-top; plot about saving the world from an STD bomb unleashed by Moe's loony ex-mistress from WWII is ridiculous. Tired, immortal Moe resides in Trump Tower with Tibetan servants and the urns of fifteen dead wives, a cross between Bruce Wayne and Mitt Romney. Script offers historical flashbacks of Moe advising Jimmy Carter, giving Hendrix a guitar, stopping Mussolini from acquiring the bomb, and sharing a cell with Nelson Mandela. In the end, Moe takes the STD nuke for the world, polluted but alive, keeping the door open for a sequel. Embryonic first draft needs work; lame dialogue undermines all the sweaty action. If this two-thousand-year-old superhero possessed the character complexity of *Wrecking Ball*, absurd actioner would be unbeatable.

CELEBRITY CORNER WITH CAROL CHUPACK

Carol: We are so excited to have Oscar-winner Antwon Legion visiting us today. Antwon, what's the worst review you've ever received?

Legion: At London's West End, a critic from the Guardian wrote, "Antwon Legion played Hamlet last night. Hamlet lost."

Carol: Tell us your first impression of Los Angeles.

Legion: Hell is empty and all the devils are here.

Carol: Is it true you didn't have Final Draft, the screenwriting software, so you wrote the script on a roll of toilet paper?

Legion: These tall tales from my publicist have got to stop. Would you read a script on 2-ply Charmin? It is true I couldn't afford Final Draft. What I would do is go into the Apple store at the Grove and write on their laptops until it closed.

Carol: I heard your Oscar-winning script about a streetwise heroin addict was originally called "Black Tar Baby."

Legion: A tar baby, as I understood it, was a doll made of tar and turpentine that was used by the racist Uncle Remus to capture the cartoon character Br'er Rabbit. The more you played with the tar baby, the more entangled you would get, that's why it's called a "sticky situation."

Carol: I watched all of your films. Do you have a Christ complex?

Legion: Just because I'm about to play Jesus doesn't make me a messiah.

Carol: The Romans called Jesus "King of the Jews." What's it like to be the King of the Industry?

Legion: My kingdom is not of this Earth.

Carol: What do you say to critics who don't want to see you play Jesus?

Legion: I say, "Qui sta la sapienza. Chi ha intelligenza, fargli contare il numero della bestia; perché è il numero di uomo: e il suo numero è seicento sessanta e sei."

Carol: My readers are curious about the afterlife. Does Hell exist?

Legion: That's for me to know and you to find out.

CARAVAGGIO'S DEPOSITION

SUPERIOR COURT OF THE STATE OF CALIFORNIA

FOR THE COUNTY OF LOS ANGELES

Signet Bank, et al.,
Plaintiffs,

No. SCU78908

VS.

CERTIFIED
COPY

LESTER BARNES,
an Individual, et
al.,
Defendant

_____

DEPOSITION OF LESTER W. BARNES

Beverly Hills, California

Wednesday, July 8, 2013

Volume 1

Reported by
MURIAL T. CARAVAGGIO
CSR No. 6969
Job No. 590202

221

ESQUIRE DEPOSITION SERVICES

Q How are we today, Mr. Barnes?

A I'm fine. I can't say how you are doing, for all I know your wife has left you and your children have stopped talking to you.

Q What was your reaction to the death of Libra Livingstone?

A I thought about the last time I saw her. We had a threesome with some Polish girl and Libra wanted me to take her shopping at Barney's.

Q Was that something you did regularly?

A Shopping? Or paying for sex?

Q Answer the question.

A Which one? Threesomes or Barney's?

Q Did you participate in an orgy with Libra Livingstone at Benny Pantera's house in Bel Air?

A My memory is a little fuzzy but I think she wore a blindfold.

Q Can you recall the names of the other men there that day?

A I would never name names. Bramley Nazarian, Rodney Muir, Walter Nikolovski, Jerry Makos, and Arthur Livingstone.

Q How many times a week did you pay Libra for sex?

A Twice a week, never on weekends. Saturdays and Sundays were spent with the ball and chain. Mostly mornings with no staff meetings.

Q At your office in Beverly Hills?

A In my Bentley, in the elevator, at this hotel I liked on Wilshire, I forget the name of it, the Sixty-Nine? I remember one time waving at a Fox executive in the parking lot at the Riv while Libra was giving me head.

Q How much did Libra charge you?

A Five hundred bucks here, five hundred there, anytime she needed something, new tires, furniture for her apartment, I paid for it.

Q Would you say you had a hooker habit?

A That money changed hands every time we saw each other was inconsequential. Libra needed money the way I needed attention.

Q Which was?

A Desperately. And I liked the way she smelled.

Q I'd like to ask you about a dark chapter in the agency's history, and there are many, but one in particular stands out for its savagery.

A I had nothing to do with year-end bonuses. That was all Arthur, talk to him.

Q What was your involvement with the assassination game known as KAOS?

A We lost a lot of decent people. I blame the janitors. They had the keys to our offices.

I watched them burn effigies in the streets of Century City. You couldn't eat anywhere without thinking about the poisonings at The Grill. That was the worst.

Q You retaliated and the janitors fought back with drive-by shootings. What started this war, does anybody even remember?

A Larry Mersault was approached by a member of facilities, the building manager who was close to the car wash guys, the automotive department, and those illegals who cleaned our offices every night. This African crime lord took my reader to lunch at Addis Ababa on Fairfax. Have you ever eaten Ethiopian food? No forks. You eat with your fingers. You think you drink from a water bowl at the table and it's for washing your hands. The African told Larry he had a film fund from janitors all over Los Angeles, not just the Omniscience/Ragnarök gang, but the life savings of every cleaner from Boyle Heights to Santa Monica. Larry thought it was drug money or some criminal enterprise, so he brought them to our Independent Film Division as a retainer client and they ended up cofinancing *Plasma Sluts* with Bellerophon Pictures.

Q Wouldn't you be upset if your life savings went into a piece of trash called *Plasma Sluts*?

A The original title was *Somebody's Daughter*, which didn't translate well overseas. If it wasn't for Larry Mersault, we wouldn't have had the Ojai Accords, which stopped the killings and outlined a general framework for peace.

Q Benny Pantera recently threw you a bachelor party where Libra Livingstone provided the entertainment.

A That's not accurate.

Q Who was the bachelor party for?

A There's never a groom. Benny just likes the ritual.

Q I want to show you a security cam video of Arthur Livingstone at one of his bachelor parties.

(clip plays)

(One angle. One room. One bed. 3:33 a.m. We are in Benny Pantera's master bedroom in Bel Air. Blindfolded, grinning, a naked Arthur Livingstone lies on his back, monstrous erection, on top of the duvet, caressed by five young naked women. No one is aware they are being recorded. The women kiss Arthur all over, don blue surgical latex gloves, straddle, rub, suckle, then abruptly, they all leave the room; a young woman in crotchless lingerie enters, smoking a crack pipe, visibly out of her head, squats onto the blindfolded man's penis after squirting her fingers with gel and shoving them between her thighs. The hard landing causes Arthur and the young woman to scream at the same time. Still inside her, Arthur lifts up his blindfold and recognizes his daughter—)

(clip ends)

A I think that was the end of Arthur's deceptive sexual-relational-compulsivity reality.

GLOW JOBS

OMNISCIENCE/RAGNARÖK SCRIPT GURU STAKES VALLEY VAMPIRES

LARRY MERSAULT FOUND FOOTAGE AT VALLEY FORGE IN THØR ROSENTHAL'S "DARK WINTER"

For Larry Mersault, the head of Omniscience/Ragnarök's story department, it was a call girl rather than a coverage that led him to the splatter-piece "Dark Winter."

"I used to drive prostitutes around L.A. before I started in the movie business. One of my girls got the lead in a film called *Plasma Sluts* by **Thør Rosenthal**. The set was like a Terry Gilliam movie," says Mersault. "I got an e-mail from Thør asking me to read this contained horror script he could make for a price on his uncle's farm near Thousand Oaks." Impressed by the no-budget auteur, Mersault raised the coin, supervised production, and steered the sale of *Dark Winter* to distributor **A24**.

"It should have been called Simi Valley Forge*," jokes Mersault. For Rosenthal, it's his first time playing in theatres. "No more hotel room premieres for me," says the North Hollywood helmer, "no more fast-forwarding my movies."

Simi Valley Forge

"No meat! No meat!" cries a soldier, ravenous, holding his belly. "Shut up Wilson!" shouts a rebel, scared he might be next. Starving Revolutionary War grunts huddle around a campfire at midnight, shivering in their long johns and frayed coats, drawn faces making them appear as animated corpses. The soldiers stumble over a rectangular crate covered with snow in the corner of a barn somewhere on a farm. Wiping away the frost, they realize the crate is a coffin with Cyrillic markings when a vampire leaps into the frame and claws their throats open, blood squirting from rubber tubing, death throes gurgling, unable to warn the others about the Strigoi slurping at the jugular fountain. A soldier enters the shot and strikes a threatening martial arts pose—

"Those were my men, Baron Friedrich Wilhelm Ludolf Gerhard Augustin von Steuben, not your dinner!"

A light shower of Gold Medal flour shakes through the air from the rafters of a distressed farmhouse off Ventura Boulevard in Thousand Oaks. The hut floor is covered in so much flour if it rained they could make enough gruel to feed the entire Revolutionary Army at the real Valley Forge.

"Cut!" screams Thør Rosenthal. "Is that a burrito wrapper in the shot?"

The offending Baja Fresh wax paper is thrown away by a skinny PA wearing a Lucio Fulci's *Zombie* T-shirt. An exasperated Thør turns to his cinematographer, who lights up a smoke: "We got it."

(Below-the-line troopers, young, exhausted, devoted to their director, arrive on set with wheelbarrows of one-pound bricks of Gold Medal flour, shaking out "snow" all over the shed until the chain-smoking production designer is satisfied.)

"Moving on!" shouts the first AD. "Scene seventy-eight!"

Lips stained orange from stuffing his face with handfuls of Cheetos, Larry Mersault hangs out by the snack table, amazed at this ninety-nine-cent recreation of Valley Forge in Southern California.

"Craft service table is for the crew," says Martha Washington, dressed in a Revolutionary War outfit.

Mersault: "Are they shooting your death scene next?"

"I don't have a death scene. I'm the star," says the saucy ingénue.

Mersault marvels at all the extras dressed in ragged colonial times gear; the FX guys applying claws and bald caps and white sclera contacts to transform Washington's revolutionary soldiers into "feeders."

"Quiet on the set!"

The FX mavens finish rigging the latex body suit with exposed ribcage and pulsating heart.

"Rolling!"

Thør Rosenthal notices Mersault lurking around the video village and slides the reader into his director's chair to take in the feeding scene.

"Speed!"

The SAG-eligible actors take their places and bare their teeth, ready to tear the soldier apart.

Thør: "Ready, Martha?"

Martha: "What winks and fucks like a tiger?"

"Action!"

The soldiers at Valley Forge shred open the latex skin on the victim's chest, howl at the top of their lungs, gnaw on the drippy flesh, and raise the fatty intestines between their hands. Thør encourages all of them to gorge more fervently, then he jabs a finger at "Martha," her cue to enter the frame. Shadows of violence flicker over Martha's expression of pure terror; on the video monitor, her mouth opens, but no sound comes out as she hides under a corpse and watches the creeps of Valley Forge slink away from the arrival of General George Washington flashing wooden teeth, revealing a pair of splintery fangs, giving a speech about the "dark winter."

"Cut! We got it!" says Thør.

"Moving on!" yells the first AD.

On the video monitor, Martha Washington looks into the camera and winks.

BEACH NUTS
Screenplay by Esther Rofoli

Low rent suspenser suffers from too many nameless slasher victims, too many storylines with zero thrills. In more pro hands, maybe this erotica/shark movie could have been pulled off. The third season filming of a JERSEY SHORE-type reality show collides with a Hammerhead shark attack that closes their beloved beaches so the cast members go clubbing and tanning instead. One of the cast members, Josie, starts sexting with the psycho Petrizzi and they become fuck buddies, which thrills the beach nut, who knocks off the reality stars in the house, saving the cameraman as his last victim. Idiotic exposition is perfect for this riff on reality contestants, spooned with mouthfuls of Petrizzi ranting about the golden age of scripted television versus the banality of Bravo TV. The best moment no question is when a naked Josie realizes the guy she's in bed with is the lunatic who murdered all her friends. Struggle in the sack ensues; Josie chases Petrizzi into the ocean; hungry Hammerhead ends his bloody reign. Dark script fails to exploit the shark-infested waters* for tension, and misses the real point of the script: on-line dating is scarier.

shark-infested waters

Boston, the limo driver for Omniscience/Ragnarök, extremely alert, checking for assassins, looks down the alley behind The Grill in Beverly Hills before giving the green light to Larry Mersault and Lester Barnes, who are ten minutes late for their lunch with the vice president of halitosis at Fox. Aware that every meal could be his last, Mersault sees his mentor remove the top of a magic marker before Boston goes first through the door at The Grill—

(Drive-by shootings in Beverly Hills had become as ubiquitous as jaywalking tickets. Celebrations of life held at Hollywood Forever were more popular than the cemetery screenings. A string of red carpet KAOS murders forced theater owners to lobby umpire Walter Nikolovski to declare certain areas off-limits for assassinations.)

The maître d' retrieves a pair of menus and escorts "Mr Barnes" and his guest to a choice booth against the mirrored wall. Producers call out Lester's name, drop their napkins, and rise up to pitch him projects. Lester speeds up his walk, then stops, causing Mersault to bump up against his back.

"Get your hands out of my pocket!" barks Lester.

Hispanic busboys look up from their trays. Lester ignores Joey Fatone and his business manager when a figure charges the agent with a raised spoon, which is sent clattering to the floor by a quick-thinking Lester, who runs over to a table in the middle of the room, his original target all along, where an Israeli arms dealer-producer never sees the magic marker swipe his forehead.

"You're dead, Oren," sneers Lester.

"I thought the Grill was a safe zone."

"Take it up with Nikolovski," says Lester, not giving a shit.

"Is that your witness?" Oren points at Mersault, marking him for death.

"You leave my reader out of this," says the agent.

"Well, I'm wearing a safety so fuck you."

"Safety? I don't see a safety—"

Oren opens his jacket slightly, revealing a baby blue T-shirt: I MISS THE OLD BRITNEY.

Lester stomps his foot, "You son of a bitch."

At their table, later, brass tacks, Fox exec Rodney Muir wonders: "Pay me, rape me, shit on me, I forget what the fourth fantasy was."

"Strangle me?" offers Mersault.

"That's not it. I can't remember," says Rodney.

Mersault: "Kill, Fuck, or Marry?"

Lester: "Pardon?"

Mersault: "Eva Braun. Tyler Perry. Big Bird. Which one would you kill, fuck or marry?"

Lester: "I'd rather floss my urethra with barbed wire."

Rodney: "You guys should go on Christian Mingle. I have this friend who goes on those sites. I've seen pictures of his victims. He's not discriminating—"

Lester: "You mean Brigham over at Universal?"

Mersault: "Aw, c'mon, do we have to talk about that guy?"

Rodney: "I hear Blacula's unhappy with Famke."

"Not anymore," says Lester, sniffing his corned beef, "does this smell bad to you?"

"Don't eat that sandwich," says Mersault.

The Hispanic busboys are long gone.

Sickened producers retch over their poisoned lunch plates.

The crowd at the Grill stampedes toward the exit, covering their mouths in revulsion.

Prescription glasses and dentures bathe in puddles of vomit on the floor.

"Fucking janitors*," mutters Lester.

JUSTICE FOR
JANITORS

SAVING SGT. KAMINSKY
Screenplay by Robert Riskin

Muscular WWII prestige piece is packed with gripping battle sequences and meaty characters you pray won't get wasted by the Krauts. Epic script starts explosively with the Normandy invasion, then settles down to follow a group of GIs led by the cynical Captain Schindler on a suicide mission to rescue Staff Sergeant Kaminsky, who for political reasons must be brought home to his parents in Kansas (his four brothers were killed in action*). When the soldiers locate Sergeant Kaminsky, he is devastated to learn that several of Schindler's men have lost their lives to rescue him. Last stand at a bagel factory pits our GIs against a horde of Nazi Panzers and everybody gets wiped out except for Kaminsky in the ferocious finale. Plenty of explosive action as tanks and tossed grenades keep the privates fighting, yet script could have used more dissension in combat, not with the enemy, but amongst themselves. Roles to die for are Schindler and the cowardly Kaminsky. The remaining members of the weary platoon are memorable, but not all of them make it out alive.

killed in action

CONFIRMED KILL LIST / WEEK OF 2.11.13 / KAOS

Garrett Izzo (New Line, Sharpie)

Diego Arriaga (Justice for Janitors, anthrax)

Jason Luntz (MGM, spork)

Sebastian Flynn (Lion Rock, cage drowning)

Dean Huggins (Insanely Creative, confetti bomb)

Tanya Gardner (Bellerophon Pictures, water balloon)

Ryan Marsh (Church of Scientology, banana)

Ross Voorhees (Hometown Films, roadside bomb)

Carl Skinner (Universal, whoopee-cushion)

Jennifer Zimmer (gang-raped by Justice for Janitors)

Priyanka Shaw (Overseas Film Group, drive-by shooting, funeral services TBA)

Beau Keene (7ate9, exploding cigar)

Bramley Nazarian (Omniscience/Ragnarök, silly putty garrote)

Alix Furst (Morgan Creek, pillow)

Natalie Sheekey (Maha Yoga, flour bomb)

Cleo Ravenscroft (Omniscience/Ragnarök, stuffed animal)

Alan Jimenez (Justice for Janitors, Soweto necklace)

Shelley Harkness (Sony Pictures Classics, hand-buzzer)

Ilene Gwartz (Imaginative Artists, light saber)

Stuart Epstein (Insanely Creative, firing squad)

Larry Mersault (Omniscience/Ragnarök, hammer, $10,500 reward posted by the Victims Advocacy Group, or VAG, to anyone with information leading to the arrest and conviction of Dollars Muttlan)

TRUE FIBS & OTHER LIES
Manuscript by Betsy Yarborough*

Amusing memoir behind the scenes (and under the sheets) relates Betsy's adventures filming the expensive vanity project directed by her future ex-husband Thør Rosenthal and the outrageous action scenes she endured with costar Hugo Slater. Betsy's remembrances are playful and compelling: production assistants argue over who will smear Cheese Whiz on a dog's butt so the hound will lick its ass on camera; Betsy and Hugo Slater's embarrassing sex scene that lands him in the hospital; the sushi chef slicing tuna faster instead of stopping when the director repeatedly shouts "Cut!" Highlight of memoir is when Thør whisks Betsy away to Mexico one weekend and they are snatched by narco-terrorists. The couple avoids being skinned alive when the crazed drug kingpin recognizes Betsy, begs her to sign his autograph book next to Cameron Diaz's page, and sets them free. While some memories are stronger than others, the funniest chapters are Betsy's memories of certain code-named costars and their icky sexual preferences. Told with honesty and humor, this rubber-necking of a sausage factory could be a Thør Rosenthal actioner starring Betsy Yarborough, who might think they've seen this movie before.

Betsy Yarborough

Missing actress, last seen in Santa Clarita as a guest speaker with professor-screenwriter Dollars Muttlan at College of the Canyons. If you have any information regarding her disappearance, contact www.valenciacrimesolvers.com

HIGH TIDE
Screenplay by Dollars Muttlan

Entertaining disaster movie delivers on its original premise of a madman who creates tidal waves and a scientist unjustly accused who's the only one who can stop a giant wave from demolishing California's coastline. Terrific premise has scientist Lee Hilton set up for murder by a villain who calls himself Scylla and gets blamed for creating tsunamis that wipe out entire beach communities. On the run with sexy but vulnerable blind date Rebecca, Lee must race against the threat of man-made disasters to clear his name and expose Scylla as evil industrialist Mr. Voris, whose disgraced Cowabunga project got shut down by whistleblower Lee who feared the energy-producing device was unstable. Pacing is brisk, complete with not one, not two, but three waves that provide epic thrills. Strong chemistry between Lee and Rebecca adds humor and romance to all the excitement. Winner of a script* delivers a character-driven tentpole that smacks of commercial success.

Winner of a script

Total horseshit; a glowjob; unreadable; see also Rusty Trombone, Dog in a Bathtub, Frothy Walrus.

STAR OF THE OCEAN
Scriptment by Samuel Glickstein

Outstanding period saga with a grand love story set on board the doomed Lusitania ship. Even in detailed treatment form (at 189 pages), this is already first class material. Present day wraparound story has a treasure hunter seeking a priceless diamond inside the sunken ship, but instead he finds a charcoal drawing of a gorgeous girl. Rosie, the subject of the mysterious sketch and a 101 year old survivor of the Lusitania, turns up to tell the real story of the boat and her romance with gambler Hank Lawson, who won a ticket on the Lusitania in a card game. Rosie's obnoxious fiancé Albert gives her a diamond necklace called the Star of the Ocean only to lose Rosie to the gambler. The Lusitania sinks, Hank perishes, Rosie and Albert survive but never see each other again, and she finds the sparkly diamond in Hank's coat pocket. Technically, story unfolds brilliantly with superbly drawn characters and an atmosphere evocative of its era. Huge in scope, high romance on the high seas, one for the ages* if everything falls into place.

one for the ages

You never forget your first glowjob. There's an apocryphal story about then-Omniscience summer intern Larry Mersault recommending *Star of the Ocean* after learning he had two hours to review and write the coverage. Truth be told, Mersault passed on the project, Glickstein's agent ordered him to "make it glow," and the reader changed his evaluation to a recommend without protest.

WHITE HOUSE PARTY*
Screenplay by Noel Heller

Franchise actioner combines elements of *Karate Kid* and *In the Line of Fire*. Though it sounds derivative, script has a terrific concept that's supported by an inspired execution. The straw that stirs the drink is the love-hate relationship between uptight Secret Service agent Dexter Moss and the President's obnoxious teenage son Wally. Initially, they can't stand each other but when Wally gets beat up by a bully, Dexter takes Wally to a karate class so he can defend himself. Middle makes Wally the target of a kidnapping plot by voters angered by the President's domestic policies. When they attempt to kidnap Wally at a Benihana restaurant, his buddies from karate school stage a hilarious rescue. In Act III, the White House comes under siege and it's up to Dexter to save the First Family. Memorable characters like Wally's distracted parental unit, the President of the United States, and Dexter's romantic interest Miriam, provide solid support. Nice touch at the end when Wally protects the bully who once tormented him. Meaty roles, snappy dialogue, high concept action-comedy deserves our attention. For Antwon Legion, this guy Dexter Moss reads like the next Axel Foley.

White House Party

As a thank you to the reader who found the script for his latest blockbuster, *White House Party*, Antwon Legion placed a double order of "egg rolls" to Mersault's duplex in the Fairfax district. Unfortunately, the Chinese prostitutes that morning knocked on the upper unit and fucked the shit out of the wrong guy.

AVALANCHE!
Screenplay by Pete Boykin

Unrelentingly grim true story about a doomed expedition of mountaineers caught in a snowstorm until an avalanche wipes out the rescue chopper, the adventurers, and any hope for the family members praying for their return. Based on a true story of death and despair at 28,251 feet, AVALANCHE! never soars to such heights. Most of the characters are indistinguishable stereotypes climbing a mountain between Pakistan and China, covered in gear and goggles. Only standout part is expedition leader Ray Hampton, whose cocky refusal to head back to base camp ends up sealing everyone's fate. Ending is such a downer it's hard to imagine the after-party* at the premiere of this feel-bad movie. Plotting is non-existent, family members are bland cutaways from the slaughter unleashed by the insidious K2, picking off the faceless climbers like a slasher movie. Doomed expedition is dragged down by dull exposition about rock climbing and oxygen sickness. Instead of celebrating the triumph of the human spirit, script succeeds in boring everyone to death before the avalanche finishes the job.

after-party

Your date for the AVALANCHE! premiere is a D-girl everybody has slept with including Thør Rosenthal, Arthur Livingstone, and half the female motion picture agents at Insanely Creative. You skip the movie at the TCL Chinese Theatre when she blows you in the bowels of the Hollywood and Highland parking structure and that's okay because you read the script and while the moment is shady you're not complaining about her technique, which is totally pro, her Thierry Mugler perfume invoking a prized memory of that backseat soixante-neuf at the drive-in with the love of your life, the one whose heart you broke after her father threatened you with a fatwa if you didn't end the office affair. You don't ejaculate because she orders you to save it for later, back at her place, that is, she says, if you still want to, wiping a blob of shiny sack fluid off her chinny chin chin. Sounds like a plan, you say, and the VP of Fellatio, hurt by your comment, writes you off as cavalier. Your name on the list gets you ushered past the velvet rope imprisoning a fall collection of slim, coked-out models in existential-crisis mode waiting to ride the lift to the rooftop party. You ride up in silence with your date, not smiling when your eyes connect in the ceiling mirror. The elevator doors widen and chunks of man-made snowflakes swirl around you like dust devils. Entering this freezing playpen of the damned, your view of the Hollywood sign is blocked by a huge K2 mountain enveloped in a fake ice storm. Your director of derailment snags a Cosmo off a tray, snarfs a bacon-wrapped scallop from a Sherpa-themed serving girl before ditching you to join a circle of cackling execs from Bellerophon standing on mounds of snow with protruding limbs. Trolls come up to you, tap your shoulder, and ask, "Did you like the movie? Be honest." Perched above the letters of the unlit hotel signage, Asian chick DJ cocks her headphone over one ear. "Am I the only one who finds the après-ski theme wildly inappropriate?" Nobody answers you when the rooftop shudders with a tremor. Then another, and another, as if an abominable Yeti were making an entrance. Everyone prostrates themselves on the ground, eyes downward. You drop to your knees in homage when cloven hoofs stop right in front of you. Antwon Legion barks at his bodyguards Fruity and Balthazar to pull you up on your feet so you are standing in the eye-line of the biggest movie star in the world: "Reader-guy! I feel like Fogo de Chao. Jew eat?"

NIGHTSHOOTER
Screenplay by Thurman Thonson

Disappointing thriller about a vigilante news stringer applies a hand-held aesthetic for tension and immediacy, but there isn't much of a story here, certainly not a tale of redemption; it's about a low-life criminal named Stu Broom, who'll do anything to break news stories for a local TV station and get paid. Writer seriously undercooks his concept and offers an erratic plot drizzled in speed and car crashes mixed with the public's insatiable appetite for human suffering. In this hybrid hand-held action-thriller, our nightshooter is a societal reject, mentally unhinged, hard to like, period. For Antwon Legion, there's never a moment where Stu Broom acts heroically, no partner to bounce off, no romantic peach to pursue. Mostly, it's about reckless ambition and cynical darkness. No humor, no lightness of being, not a pleasant feeling when this script ends. A shower sounds good right now*.

A shower sounds good right now

A rare personal attack from a reader who strived to achieve the perception of objectivity despite the highly subjective nature of script coverage. His dog must have died that day or, more likely, Mersault passed on *Nightshooter* ($12M budget/$88M worldwide cume) after learning about his neighbor's double order of egg rolls.

—

A.W.O.L.
Screenplay by Wayne Sheehy

Outstanding writing fuels this commercial prestige piece about a man who can't find his place in the world, an Air Force instructor who goes rogue after losing his wings and his will to live. Combining *Top Gun* aerial action with a doomed pilot similar to Denzel's troubled aviator in *Flight* makes for a mortality drama that's strangely life-affirming. Aging flyboy Mickey Rivers, a showcase role for a star, takes off in an F-16 for one final ride with best friends Harris and Dawson struggling on the ground to save their lost pilot. Harris, the cowardly desk jockey selling his soul for military stripes, ends up giving the order to have Rivers shot down. Dawson is a terrific foil, the guy who married Lourdes, a stewardess they both competed for; script hints darkly that Rivers may have preferred Dawson over Lourdes, a rumor never repeated or confirmed. Going out in a blaze of glory*, his final moments looking into the sun, Rivers provides an ending that will haunt audiences. On his flypath to destruction, story sometimes feels one-note, but that's a quibble when the people are so deeply drawn, their emotions soaring higher than any jet. Triumphant and tragic, let's champion this for our top gun clients.

blaze of glory

"A studio executive, the Anti-Christ, and a script reader walk into a club. The bartender looks at them and says: 'Get the fuck out of here!' That's it. That's the joke. Uh-huh. Uh-huh. Someone, somewhere, is tired of screwing Libra."

Studying the credits of an autographed poster of *Liquid Sky*, waiting for the head of legal affairs to finish a call, Mersault grins at a Kevlar vest (bullseye target on its back) framed in bulletproof-glass with a message from Justice for Janitors: THE BEST NIKOLOVSKI IS A DEAD NIKOLOVSKI.

Hanging up, Nikolovski turns to the reader: "Lester and I had a conversation about you the other day."

"Is that right?"

"We were discussing how to raise your profile."

The lawyer opens his desk drawer, unfolds a dusty fuck towel from Abyssinia, revealing a gem-encrusted handle of a sacrificial knife.

"Antwon Legion must die."

"Say it again?"

"You're the only one in the industry he trusts."

"And if I say no?"

"No is just a moment in time."

"Does this have anything to do with Antwon cutting his commission?"

"We don't do nickels."

"Why do I get the Sophie's Choice? I'm not even an agent."

"I've arranged for you to play Longinus, the Roman Centurion who pierces Jesus in his ribs. Someone will hand you a prop spear on set. Affixed to the blade will be this ancient secespita. You will be the next *I Am Legend* and Golgotha will be his Samarra."

"Is that like Two Bunch Palms?"

"A merchant in Baghdad sends his servant to the market square for groceries. Hours later, the servant comes back terrified, telling his master he ran into a woman he recognized as Death, and she made a frightening gesture toward him. The servant steals a horse and escapes to Samarra where he thinks Death cannot find him. The merchant goes to the market square where Death is sipping a green tea latte and demands to know why she made a menacing gesture at his servant. Death goes, 'It wasn't menacing. I was shocked to see him in Baghdad because I have a spinning class with him tomorrow in Samarra.'"

Nikolovski picks up the blade, walks around the standing desk and places a hand on Mersault's shoulder—

"You're asking me to murder my friend."

"The Academy wants this to happen."

Nikolovski jams the Nerf dagger into the reader's neck. The weapon is made of foam rubber.

"Make sure there's a witness," insists the umpire, "or the killing won't count."

Meeting over, Nikolovski offers the reader a farewell fist bump.

"You could get the Thalberg Award for this."

WE'LL ALWAYS HAVE BENGHAZI
Screenplay by Ken Kinski

Chaotic, you-are-there approach drops us right into the long dark night* of Benghazi horror, another true tale of unfriendly Arabs, siege script is more *Rambo* than *Argo*, but fact-based thriller perhaps most resembles *Aliens* (script wisely keeps the enemy vague and scary). This might not be the best Benghazi project floating out there, but it could be the first out of the gate to cover the intense siege of the U.S. embassy by terrorists on the anniversary of 9/11. For two-thirds of the script, there's tremendous action/gunfire with our guys driving around Benghazi like *The French Connection*, avoiding roadside bombs and mortar fire. For Antwon Legion, the role of Perry narrates the tale and outlives everyone; sidekick Flo-Jo is thinly written as a gun-toting cowboy; script doesn't have the chops to humanize these heroes. The challenge will be to make this noisy script resonate emotionally. Ending is pure tragedy; when it's all over, we don't feel anything but relief.

long dark night

Larry Mersault haunts the city in his Chrysler LeBaron convertible like the Flying Dutchman, squeezing the lemon at every traffic light, running stop signs as if braking would cause his heart to cease beating; asking himself, at what point did his life go sideways?

(Maybe it was that time Arthur Livingstone called his office: "Stop playing hide the Nazi with my daughter. Crush her heart so Libra will never see you again. I need you to read a script for me.")

Where would he be tonight if he had continued driving around sex workers after film school for that criminal who rented a photography studio on Ventura and Tujunga? Would he have ended up running the escort service? Mersault flashes on the entertainment delivery boss of *Sunset Strip*. What was the name of that ruthless pimp?

(Malice!)

The empire of whores had a frightening vice-president of dominoes. What was the name of that illiterate football player who played one season for the Raiders before the linebacker fractured his vertebrae?

(Roemello!)

God's lonely reader takes Fountain, left on Highland, curving into La Brea, green lights passing over his head, Venice, Jefferson, right on Stocker, left on La Cienega, signs appearing for LAX, right on La Tijera, passing the Chuck E.

Cheese's, Wing Stop, and Harriet's Soul Cuisine displaying the dreaded "C" rating from the sanitation department.

(Driving up Bronson Canyon, a hundred yards from Larry's newly acquired house in the hills, Arthur Livingstone's daughter texts her boyfriend of two months:

Libra: *I can't wait to suck your dick*

Arriving at his one-bedroom house on Tuxedo Terrace, Libra finds the front door open—

"Larry?"

No response. Letting herself in, Libra surveys the empty first floor, fifty-inch TV blasting ESPN. She climbs the stairs toward his deserted bedroom, hears water running, enters the steamy bathroom, removes her clothes and steps into the frosted glass encased shower—

The water spray doesn't stop. Neither does Mersault and the black chick he's taking from behind.

"Close the door," says Mersault, mid-thrust.

Libra collects her clothes; runs out of the bathroom; out of the house; out of his life.

"You're an icicle," says the escort from *Sunset Strip*.

"You should meet her old man.")

The Chrysler LeBaron veers away from the airport where a Southwest Airlines ticket attendant checks in an African-

American grandmother traveling on his 8:55 p.m. flight to watch her grandson play his first game at the point guard position for New Mexico State.

Right on Sepulveda, taking Lincoln Boulevard, past LMU, where Mersault taught a one-time only master class on script coverage that ended up being viewed 89,164 times on YouTube; passing Bali Way, where two roommate hookers took turns rocking his world for a year after Libra.

California Incline to PCH, no traffic at all, push the speedometer to ninety-five miles an hour, take Topanga to the 101 South, exit Van Nuys Boulevard straight to Bob's Classy Lady, pull into the parking lot, which Mersault now sees is full; the Asian bouncer in a black Regis outfit says park on the street but the reader keeps going, back on the freeway, toward the 15 East.

Decision time: head home via the 101 or Billy Wilder Boulevard? Mersault decides to fill up his tank at the next 76 station. He's got a long road ahead of him tonight; he's going to take his talents to Taos, where he'll arrive on set long after the Jonesy shot.

SHOCKER! 'GOLGOTHA' Loses Director on First Day of Production

EXCLUSIVE: On the first day of shooting indie desert thriller *Golgotha*, writer/director **Thør Rosenthal** was a no-show and replacing him behind the camera was the film's producer-star **Antwon Legion**.

Faith-based *Golgotha* tells the story of Judas Iscariot (Michael Fassbender), hired by Pontius Pilate (Seth Rogen) to investigate whether an unemployed carpenter named Jesus (Antwon Legion) is the messiah or a maniac stalking prostitutes on the streets of Jerusalem.

"We're ready to go. We've got a great script, a great crew and a superb cast," said producer **Benny Pantera**. Obviously there's more drama behind the cross than we know. **$tay tuned**.

GOLGOTHA
Screenplay by Thør Rosenthal

Hardly the greatest story ever told. Head-scratcher of a script takes a lurid, pulpy approach to the last days of Jesus Christ. Imagine *Angel Heart* with Judas as a gumshoe recruited by Pontius Pilate to investigate a Jewish carpenter claiming to be the redeemer and preaching "Love thy neighbor, turn thy cheek." What could have been a memorable mash-up of genres suffers from flowery dialogue and iconic biblical characters trapped in a bad pastiche of Mickey Spillane. Low point of the script is a gratuitous orgy sequence with the fraternal disciples and a totally game Mary Magdalene. Middle has a grim subplot of Barabbas stalking prostitutes and leaving their heads in a baptismal lake to be discovered by devout followers. Judas ends up saving Mary Magdalene, but it's Jesus, not Barabbas, who is condemned by the bloodthirsty crowd. Intriguing faith-based noir, wobbly script, *Last Temptation* meets *Se7en**, it's not the savior that deserves crucifixion.

Last Temptation meets *Se7en*

Red and pink static in a circle, eye of an electromagnetic field, a mackerel sky; BOSE headphones over a crown of thorns blasts Creed's "*My Own Prison*" in Legion's ears. A camera assistant catches the flicked-away headphones, holds up a monitor on a selfie stick to an immobile Legion on the gore-soaked lumber, awaiting approval.

"Let's do this," says the redeemer-director.

All those on set steel themselves to shoot the crucifixion in a single, uninterrupted take.

First AD queries the crew: "Is everybody ready?"

(Earlier, in the garden of Gesthemane, Legion huddles with his followers, giving them props for enduring the last forty days in the desert: "I say to you today you will be with me in paradise," leading them with the morning chant for the last time: "Say who, say ha! Say who, say ha! Say who, who, who, 1-2-3-GOLGOTHA!")

"Speed," yells the sound recordist, followed by "Camera A rolling!" and "Camera B rolling!"

The clapper loader fills the frame with a digital slate: 'Scene two twenty eight, take one."

The first AD bellows: "Action!"

Start on Legion's exposed ribcage.

"Father, forgive them, for they know not what they do!"

Legion turns to the thieves Gestas and Dismas execrating God for their crucifixion.

"I thirst!" cries Legion, his eye-line clear, storm clouds in the distance.

Extras raise a sponge dipped in sour wine on a sprig of hyssop to the star's parched lips.

The one-take bravura shot continues.

Legion recognizes Larry Mersault playing a Roman centurion among the crowd of local hires, reluctant expression on his face, unclean blade attached to his pike.

All at once, the set disappears.

The sun is no more.

Gestas and Dismas, gone.

The extras.

The trailers.

The camera equipment.

The camera operator.

The focus puller.

All gone, as if making movies never existed.

Legion: "My God, my God, why have you forsaken me?"

Shafts of sunlight knife through aboriginal darkness.

Gestas and Dismas reappear, cursing their predicament.

With spear of destiny upturned, the extra-turned-assassin Larry Mersault makes his move.

Everyone is back on set.

The epic one-take shot pulled off.

Mersault: "You're dead, Antwon."

Only then does the biggest movie star in the world unleash a thousand watt smile.

"It is accomplished—"

JESUS ACTOR STRUCK BY LIGHTNING

ANTWON LEGION HAS DIED ON DESERT THRILLER SET

The film has been canceled following the death of Golgotha's director, producer, and star. "Antwon Legion is finally unavailable," said agent Lester Barnes in a statement. "He leaves us one unfinished masterpiece and tons of regrets."

ANTWON LEGION

The lightning bolt killed the actor and injured an extra portraying a Roman centurion. "Get off the cross, Antwon. They need the wood," said the extra Larry Mersault, who suffered light burns to his hands. "Seriously, you will be missed."

Golgotha's co-writer Thør Rosenthal had the last word about the messianic star: "Why would God be so mad at Antwon Legion playing his son in a movie unless he totally disagreed with the casting?"

FRANKIE GOES TO HOLLYWOOD
Revised by Andrew Dufresne

Outstanding rewrite, perversely macabre retelling of *The Modern Prometheus* paints Viktor Frankenstein as an ambitious dental assistant who assists a mad orthodontist named Igor (a welcome reversal of roles) in resurrecting the dead, failing repeatedly until they succeed wildly with raising a mean girl corpse named "Frankie." Viktor and Igor become fearful parents to their monstrous child, hiding her in the bowels of a South Robertson medical building. Frankie rebels when she realizes her body is made up of stolen parts; her entitled teenage brain, however, transforms her into a ghastly monster. There's an extraordinary classroom scene when a sympathetic Fairfax High teacher tries to help Frankie answer a basic geography question, and the teen corpse murders the instructor in a fit of rage. Frankie is tormented by her lack of memories and existential shame. One of the script's many highlights is the corpse's gentle nature, her deep longing for affection underneath the scarred exterior. Viktor, Igor, and the Monster come alive (*alive!*) on the page. The talk* is marvelous. Darkly compelling, *Heathers* meets *Young Frankenstein*, a Gothic popcorn movie for the masses.

The talk

Larry Mersault peers over a podium at the rows of mostly Hispanic family members waving glue-glittered signs inside the Arthur J. Livingstone Auditorium. The student body texts away, lit up by iPhones, oblivious to the significance of this life chapter event. Projected on the curtains behind the commencement speaker are the words ABANDON ALL HOPE YE WHO EXIT HERE.

"First of all, I want to congratulate the class of 2013."

(*applause*)

"I want to thank the prestigious Los Angeles Film School for inviting me to be your graduation speaker. I heard Roman Polanski was not available."

(*silence*)

Larry Mersault places a Chivas Regal bag on the podium. He yanks down the purple velvet like a tube top, revealing a golden Oscar statuette. Sharing his triumph with the graduates—

"I had to kill someone to get this."

(*laughter*)

"This Honorary Oscar recognizes extraordinary distinction in lifetime achievement, or exceptional contributions to motion picture arts and sciences, or outstanding service to the Academy. I wanted the Thalberg."

(*applause*)

"All of you are going to Hell. Most definitely, as Dwyane Wade would say. Now, Hell is not 'other people' as said by Jean-Paul Camus. Hell is where the glasses have holes in them and the women don't. When Saint Peter shows you a video and Hell looks fantastic, don't believe him, it's the trailer. Our receptionist, who I am no longer fucking, that's a joke, she plays for the other team, told me yesterday she is leaving the business because she doesn't know who she is anymore. That is an excellent reason for leaving any business."

(*silence*)

"Hot tip number one: figure out what you like to do and do it well. Do it for free. Find a place to do it. Do it for money. Do it all night for money and you're a professional."

(*silence*)

"Let me get back to Hell, I mean, the movie business, the industry, the Coliseum you are about to enter. I watched Ridley Scott's *Gladiator* on Netflix last night. What did the studio executive say to the screenwriter who first pitched the idea of Maximus? I'll never say who it was, but Rodney Muir at Fox had this brilliant note for David Franzoni: 'Does he have to be a gladiator? What if Maximus was a janitor who cleans toilets and gets into gladiator school?' There's one scene in that movie that sums up what the industry is really like. The gladiators are all standing in darkness under the Coliseum, the stadium chanting for their deaths, the guy next to Maximus vomits all over the guy in front of him, another gladiator pisses himself, one guy, eyes wide, looks like a total madman, probably can't wait to get out there and start killing, and then there's Maximus, steady as a fucking rock. Be that guy."

(*silence*)

"Tip number two: get a mentor. That's the whole ball game. Find that nine hundred pound mentor and perform any task that is asked, no matter how demeaning, and that gorilla will one day make a life-changing phone call to Alan Horn on your behalf."

(*silence*)

"Tip number three: find someone to share your life with or you will die alone, your mummified body discovered by police after a neighbor calls for a welfare check."

(*silence*)

"Number four: have children. They help to ease the boredom."

(*laughter*)

"Nugget number five: be the best friend you can be and your friends will be your family."

(*applause*)

"I did none of those things. I have no friends. I sold my soul to a movie star. I used to read for a talent agency. Now

I work for a media hydra representing GMO corporations, asymmetrical militant extremists, and Chobani yogurt."

(*silence*)

"If I have one regret in this life I should have said 'yes' to that Irish chick who invited me to her hotel room after we had dinner at Sushi on Sunset but she was married to the Irish ambassador and I chose not to upset the Belfast Peace Agreement."

(*applause*)

"And finally, to the graduates of the Los Angeles Film School, my last bit of advice for all of you about to enter the industry: don't do it."

Author photo by Lawrence Raymond

Adam Novak is the author of the novels *The Non-Pro* and *Take Fountain*. He lives and writes in Los Angeles, California.

VERY SPECIAL THANKS

Lauren, Sara, Tabitha & Doctor Bombay, Reinhard, Greathouse, André, Cox, the Fisch, Jason, Jen, Lockhart, John Ptak, Brent Morley, WME, and J.D.

Mom, Dad, Jonathan, Barbara and Brian—your tough love rescued the novel from the abyss.

Henry Bean, Miranda Van Iderstein, and Nancy Guan—the best notes I've ever seen, and that's saying something.

Tyson, Alice, Julia, Hailie, and Andrew at Rare Bird Books—for your patience, for your passion, and for publishing me.